William Shakespeare said All the world's a stage, but he hadn't counted on shifters under a theater's hot lights. Lovers Sam Hightower and Grant Newsome live for the stage. Although they have enjoyed the wanderlust of traveling theater for many years, each has grown tired of the road and wants to settle down. They also have a secret. As shifters and no part of any pack, they are lone wolves in every sense of the word. The full moon brings out the beast in them.

Even though their work as gaffers—lighting techs—puts them in contact with a large variety of willing, sexy men and women to share their love, they prefer men. They find a dancer, Luke Pearce, who makes their blood run hot, but Luke has a secret of his own to test them. Add scenic artists and lovers Charlotte and Lina to the mix, and you have a wild and sexy fivesome.

To spoil their fun and to their surprise, Sam and Grant discover another shifter in their midst, but this young person is so inexperienced and terrified she could expose them to the human hunters and get them killed. How can Sam and Grant protect themselves as well as the people they love?

Full Moon Fever
Copyright © 2020 Elizabeth Black
ISBN: 978-1-4874-2751-1
Cover art by Martine Jardin

Published by eXtasy Books Inc or
Devine Destinies, an imprint of eXtasy Books Inc

Look for us online at:
www.eXtasybooks.com or www.devinedestinies.com

Full Moon Fever

By

Elizabeth Black

DEDICATION

I could not have written this book without support from my husband, son, family, and friends. I'd also like to thank those who helped and befriended me during my stage tech years when I worked as a gaffer in lighting, scenic artist, and FX makeup artist for stage, TV, movies, and concerts. I'd also like to thank my editors, cover artist, and eXtasy Books for publishing my novel. Without the support from and history with all these people, this book would never have been written.

CHAPTER ONE

Stage Screw (n): A large screw that is screwed through the foot of a stage brace to secure it to a strong wooden floor. Do not use in a theater with fine wood flooring.
Screw (v): To have sexual intercourse.

Sam Hightower tightened a Fresnel on a light tree as he watched the dancers warm up. He stood somewhat hidden in the wings, a position where he could observe the stage without being noticed. He preferred his life that way — out of sight, out of mind. He liked to blend into the shadows, keeping a safe distance, since his stay in the theater company was so fleeting.

At a height of six-feet-one inch and as lean as a whippet, Sam struck a powerful first impression. His thick blond hair fell to slightly below his shoulder blades. While he worked the lights, he wore it tied back and out of his way. Muscular and slim with an angular face and blue eyes, his Nordic features turned the heads of both men and women alike. Although he played both sides of the field, he preferred men. With each show, he and his partner, Grant Newsome, grew closer together, bonding with intensity only two men with deep secrets could. Sam feared their secrets could become their undoing on each leg of their tour, especially during the full moon. So far, they'd lucked out. No one had caught on to what they really were.

As was the nature of the traveling stage shows, his time in

Portland, Oregon would not last long, even though they were in the same city as their home base. He and Grant had been among the few stagehands who traveled with the company for its North American tour. The remainder for each show was filled with local crews.

Sam could see the entire country and not make a commitment to stay in any one location. Jumping from city to city was also safer, since there was little to no danger of the locals finding out that they sought the moon each month.

He and Grant had jumped at the chance to tour the Pacific Northwest and immediately joined the tour to stay close to home. In all tours, relationships between crew, actors, and dancers grew quickly with great intensity, but once the curtain fell for good, some of the cast and crew would part ways, sometimes to never to see each other again. While the split at the end was always painful, Sam willingly chose that way. He thought it best he never became too close to anyone except Grant. Grant had been his bright island oasis, a refuge from day-to-day troubles. However, such solitude begot loneliness, so they liked to share their love with a third or even fourth partner on occasion, and Sam was on the lookout for one at that very moment.

The man who flowed across the stage with such little effort looked so much like Grant that Sam blinked his eyes to make sure his vision wasn't playing tricks on him. His pulse raced at the sight of the dancer's ripped abs, shock of dark hair, and tight thighs.

Who's the god who has the rapt attention of every man and woman in this room?

Grant's twin wore his hair shoulder length, thick and full, with tendrils falling in his shining green eyes.

Those eyes are emerald green, so green they glow like an aurora in winter

His face bore a smoldering look of extreme concentration. Sam suspected this man would snap at him, turning on him in an instant if he interrupted his train of thought, much the same way Grant grumbled if Sam interrupted him. His grace could not hide the raw masculinity that moved with each muscle. Broad shoulders and muscular arms tapered to a narrow waist and an ass that threatened to slip out of the leotard he wore. Sam enjoyed gazing at that ass as the dancer soared across the stage. He preferred taut gluts to any other part of a man's body.

The man's resemblance to Grant intrigued Sam. Was he a tiger between the sheets the way Grant was? How could he approach him to find out? Considering the higher percentage of gays and lesbians in theater, there was a good chance the dancer would be amenable to a little male flirtation and maybe more. He wore the same dark and somewhat angry expression of intensity Grant wore when he concentrated on focusing lights. He smoldered like lightning in a crackling sky.

Each twist of the dancer's hips enhanced the sensuality his meager leotard couldn't contain. He strutted amid his shorter and less stellar-looking partners and brought a flush to Sam's cheeks. He moved with grace befitting a dancer, and animal magnetism oozed from his every pore. Grant's arms were fuller and stronger than the dancer's from his years of experience hauling lights, but the resemblance between the two men could not be missed. Strong and majestic, the power of this man's sexuality seeped from every pore, his potent form so beautiful it took Sam's breath away.

A sultry and husky feminine voice jarred Sam from his daydream. "Sorry, luv, you're a day late and a dollar short. We've already had him." Charlotte stood before him with her arms akimbo and a hip thrust out, giving him a cheeky grin. Covered with splatters of paint befitting her job as a scenic artist, she brandished a brush in one hand.

Charlotte was tall for a woman. At five feet and ten inches

and build like Wonder Woman on steroids, Charlotte could probably throttle Sam with those strong hands, but her slender body was not overwhelmed with bulk the way bodybuilders were. She was a nice combination of brawn and sleekness. Dressed in tight black jeans and a tighter black tank top that squeezed together her huge breasts, she twisted her bee-stung lips in an amused grin that told him she had once again bested him in the fucking department. "His name's Leuker Pearce, and he's a stallion in bed."

"I'd love to pierce him," Sam said.

"You might be able to," Lina said.

Like Sam and Grant, Lina and Charlotte were lovers. The quieter of the two scenic artists stood behind Charlotte, her arms wrapped around the gutsier one's waist. Although Lina was about two inches shorter than Charlotte, the two women could have been identical twins. What was it with the doppelgänger twins in this company? They wore their coffee-colored hair tied back, and their ponytails fell to the middle of their backs. Skin the color of espresso with a heavy dollop of cream, they stood out amid all the blondes, ordinary looking brunettes, and oddball blue and pink-haired in the crew. Their personalities offset each other's, Lina's air to Charlotte's fire. Slow to excite, Lina often corralled Charlotte's exuberance. She kept her fiery twin calm and somewhat sensible.

Quite the virago, Charlotte had thrilled Sam with her lusty nature on the few occasions they'd found themselves in bed together. Or in the back seat of his car. Or those two times in the catwalks when their groans had echoed throughout the theater. Charlotte preferred women to men, but Sam had enjoyed her touch and smell too many times to count.

He often teased her by sneaking up on her and grabbing her boobs. She retaliated by bursting unexpectedly from behind road boxes and squeezing his cock. Despite the sex play, they were buddies more than lovers.

Sam could never get away with such behavior with Lina. Quieter than Charlotte, she bordered on being shy, which made Charlotte's vibrancy seem even more pronounced. She preferred to keep to herself while Charlotte played the social butterfly. Despite her standoffishness, her intensity of concentration and conversation often surprised those who didn't know her well. It was a mistake to think of her as a shrinking violet.

Her physique was slimmer than Charlotte's and made her seem shorter than she actually was. Both women had hourglass figures with an emphasis on their large breasts and rounded asses. Once again, Sam found himself attracted to their bottoms. These two women were perfectly proportioned, something he had not seen very often. They were nearly geometrically perfect.

Still amazed at how much the two women looked alike, Sam admired their sleek arms and hands, strong from years of painting sets. Charlotte and Lina had been traveling with the troupe since its inception. They had moved from the Calvert Beach apartments in Delaware to a suburb of Washington, D.C. to get in on the stage action and made no secret about looking for greener pastures in the northwest areas once the tour was finished.

Sam and Grant had met them after their third show. The women had joined the stagehand's union at the same time Sam and Grant did, and they soon found themselves on many of the same tours together, which was unusual for traveling stage shows

While Sam could hoist a light and even design some lighting for sets, Charlotte and Lina were true artists. Their talent never ceased to impress him. Sam had seen them render flats into three-dimensional paintings. He had seen Charlotte turn an ordinary chair into a masterpiece of paint designed to look like wood with beautiful fabric seats for a show set in the late

1800s. She also painted portraits in her private time and sold them for a tidy sum. Lina sculpted from clay and bronze, mostly the human body, especially women with strong physiques. Rich people from around the country often commissioned her sculptures for their own private collections, and she brought in a mint with her impressive talent.

Sam knew he could never compete in the talent department with those two. He didn't have an artistic bone in his body. Neither did Grant. Sam could barely draw stick figures. Watching Charlotte and Lina create beautiful paintings and sculptures from what seemed like thin air impressed Sam so much he constantly reminded them how talented they were when they were hard on themselves, which was often. Such was the life of an artist. Constant self-criticism.

Sam looked to where his lover's twin writhed before him, making love to the stage as he twirled and leaped.

Imagine the threesome we could have. It would be like something out of a Penthouse letter.

"He swings both ways," Charlotte said. "I can see a hot little threesome there—you, Luke, and Luke's ravishing twin. You need to be adventurous. You know how much I love adventure."

Should he expound on that fantasy ménage? No, not just yet. "So you noticed the resemblance, too?" Lust tingled the hairs on the back of Sam's neck. That beautiful creature moved like a majestic buck in the Alaskan high country. "What kind of name is Leuker?"

"It's Dutch. It's also his middle name. Says his first name is horrible."

"Leuker isn't?"

Her deep, throaty laugh reverberated among the flats. "He goes by Luke. He told me Leuker is his mother's maiden name. Says it means good-looking."

Sam gawked at the tight ass and strong legs that sashayed across the stage. "Can't deny that." He wiped one hand across his forehead, fighting off his arousal. "Is he Carl's replacement?"

Carl had dislocated his knee during a recent practice, ending his time as lead male dancer. In a panic, the director contacted the next man on the list to take the part.

"Yes. He arrived last night."

Grant walked toward them carrying two Fresnel stage lamps. His shoulder length dark brown hair fell in waves away from his face. Shorter than Sam by about three inches, he made up for it with his strong physique. While Sam was tall and muscular, Grant was shorter but just as powerfully built. His muscles, especially in his arms, had grown in his four years lifting lights and shoving around road crew boxes. He was dark to Sam's light not only in appearance but in personality. While Sam was more cheerful and sometimes downright silly, Grant could be a cantankerous man. His resting face was a scowl, and he wasn't even angry. His general facial expressions sometimes put people off, but he knew it, so he made a point of greeting the wary with a big smile. His cheeky grins always diffused uncomfortable situations.

Grant smiled as he approached Sam, biceps bulging with the weight of the lamps, which were bulky, oblong, and metal weighing fifteen pounds each. "Sure could use some help here, lover," he snarled, winking at Sam to let him know he wasn't angry.

"He's talking to us. We were noticing how much the lead dancer looks like you, and *we've* already had him." Charlotte rubbed Grant's arm. "Your biceps are huge."

"It's from hoisting lights every day. You two have been on this tour only four months, and you've already gone through nearly every actor and actress. Now you're working on the dance troupes?"

"Time to play catch-up, Grant," Lina said. "You've been touring for six months, and we're way ahead of you." Lina's lips parted as she absent-mindedly fingered her ponytail.

"The three of you would look awesome together. It would be like Narcissus and his reflection in the water," Charlotte said.

"*He's* the one we're talking about." Sam nodded toward Leuker. "He could be your younger brother. I could tear his leotard off him and take him right there on the stage. Followed by you. Even though Charlotte and Lina already beat us to him, we might stand a chance. He bats for both teams."

"It's oddly intriguing. Imagine me making love to my mirror image. Is he game for a threesome?" Grant asked.

"He could be," Charlotte said. "I've seen him eyeing up Sam."

Grant's congenial laugh warmed Sam's heart. "We're more beastly than he knows."

Even though Sam and Grant liked and trusted Charlotte and Lina, they had not told the women the secret they kept from everyone. There was no point in telling them. All four were nomads, with the tour never remaining in one location for long during the season.

As Charlotte and Lina walked off to paint the set, Sam eyed up at the moon peeking at him from outside the window. "We have to be careful. It's hunting season, and they're out in droves now. It's dangerous out there."

"I agree. Worst time for a full moon." Grant said. "No matter where we are, we end up hiding from the locals when the full moon comes out. At least this month we're in familiar country."

At the sight of the sadness in Grant's eyes, Sam's jocular mood dampened. As lone wolves in every sense of the word, they did not belong to a pack. The life of the theater was ideal for them. If they risked exposure of their uncontrollable feral nature for some reason, they uprooted and fled to a new location. For the last few years, when not traipsing around the country dressed in black and brandishing nine-inch crescent wrenches, they resided in a townhouse in Portland, Oregon. A two-story affair, the home sat at a secluded end of a cul-de-sac. The front faced the street, and the back faced the woods.

Since road shows were held mostly over the spring, summer, and early fall, they retired to their private hideaway during the winter. Their neighbors were friendly, but they kept a safe and polite distance. Neither Sam nor Grant knew any of them well.

The two lovers celebrated Christmas every year with a gigantic blue spruce tree and ornaments they had collected together over the years. Neither man had surviving family, and when their parents and siblings were alive, they had not lived in the area. The two weren't always alone over the holidays. Charlotte and Lina, the only two he and Grant liked, had joined them over the past two Christmases and Thanksgivings. Sadly, they didn't invite them over enough when home for the winter.

They mostly kept to themselves, which was how they wanted it. No pack behavior for them. They found packs to be filled with pretentious asshats who were too full of themselves for their own good. Sam had never met a Lycan in a pack he could tolerate over dinner and drinks.

The only regret Sam had was he could not own a cat. He loved cats, but it would be cruel to adopt one or two and leave them with the neighbors for months on end when he was on the road. How he wished for a cat! Two kitties, preferably, so they had someone to play with.

He knew Grant missed growing herbs, peppers, and vegetables in a private garden in the back yard. 'Couldn't grow plants outside in the dead of winter. The man had a green thumb, except he could never seem to get seeds to germinate in the house beneath plant lights. Grant enjoyed life on the road, constantly on the move, but Sam had grown weary of it.

For once, why can't we stay put?

"I know you're tired of running, lover. We need to talk about that." Grant cupped Sam's face with one hand. "I know just the place for us. I found a cave last night. We can hide there for the next few days when we aren't working if we can't make it home. You drinking the tea?"

Sam closed his eyes and rested his cheek against his lover's grizzled jaw. "Yeah. It's helping, but I'm going to shift no matter what."

Grant had become Lycan in 1931 while vacationing in Freiberg, Germany. After much trial and error, he'd developed a concoction of savory herbs in a base of rye liquor that kept his shifting at bay to the point that he could control it. He experimented with monkshood, the number one herb that fended off werewolves, and soon added the bright red berries of mountain ash.

Over Christmastime, he often added mistletoe leaves and berries for kicks, and because it was hard to find the mistletoe any other time of year. He added spearmint, lemon balm, and peppermint to kill the horrible taste. The monkshood and rye swill tasted like graveyard dirt, but it controlled his shifting into wolf form enough to keep him out of trouble.

Without the drink, they would shift completely. Although it was noxious, they forced it down, so their limbs lengthened only a touch and their eyes shone bright yellow, but nothing more.

The last thing Sam wanted to do was explain why he turned Big Bad Wolf every month. The rye drink helped tone down his shifting, but he was worried about the hunters. He didn't want to be shot.

Sam and Grant spent the next half hour hoisting lamps onto beams from the precarious perch of ladders. Nothing could be better than working together—light touches while passing each other on the catwalks, a quick and passionate kiss behind the flats, a pat on the ass when standing on a ladder, as Grant had just done to Sam, who jumped in surprise at the swat.

Both Sam and Grant wore black denim designer jeans and black t-shirts with the show's name and *Local Crew* stamped on the left breast. Dressed in black, they blended into their surroundings so well they could grope each other without being seen.

Socket wrenches, crescent wrenches, black rope ties, and diagonal cutters hung from their belts. Ever wary of heavy equipment falling on their feet, they wore steel-toed boots. For safety reasons, Sam wore his long hair in a ponytail. Occasionally he wore a black baseball cap, but not today.

With the new cast and crew rummaging about the stage, Sam wondered who he and Grant would share their lusts with during this particular tour. There were so many delectable men and women, but Sam, as well as Grant, preferred a strapping boy toy to occupy their time and their bed.

Their past lovers had included an Italian baritone with a voice so rich it made Sam's knees knock. When the man-made love to him and Grant, he often sang arias in Italian at the top of his lungs to show his excitement. Grant hated when he did that, which only inspired the man to do it more often.

Two years ago, they'd worked an east coast tour of *A Streetcar Named Desire*. The man who played Stanley Kowalski was a big brute of a hulk who looked like he could beat up the Hell's Angels. The first time Sam and Grant bedded him, he revealed himself to be a very tender and caring lover with a shy streak, totally unlike the beast he played on stage. He collected antique miniature soldiers and rare books. Grant was delighted to learn he had designed his own garden, and the two men could talk growing vegetables and fruit trees for hours.

Women also found their way into their bed, especially buxom brunettes. Both of them never turned down a woman with hair the color of chestnuts and firm bodies with plenty of curves. Neither man liked waifs, nor did these gentlemen prefer blonds. They often enjoyed two and sometimes three lovers per tour. The man Sam had his eye on for this tour was special in more ways than his ability to flex his body like a pretzel.

As Sam lifted a light, Leuker stretched his back and legs, loosening up a tight hamstring. Muscles in his back flexed and pulsed with each bend. It took all of Sam's effort not to let out an approving and aroused groan. The advantage to being gay in the theater was he didn't find it necessary to hide his sexual nature from his colleagues and friends. Gay, lesbian, bi, trans, all were not only accepted amid the hot lights and grease-paint, they were not even given a second thought. Total acceptance, which was not nearly as common in the outside straight world. Sam could admire the masculine form on stage with ease and confidence rather than hide his desire as he would in the straight *normal* world.

What would Leuker think of Sam's proposal that they share some time together with Grant? Sam doubted he'd be offended, since he was certain the dancer had been approached often during every show. He might even be flattered. You never knew. Relationships in the theater tended to be rather fluid, so Sam suspected his request wouldn't be met with eyebrows raised in indignation.

Sam had made the mistake of propositioning once during a tour. The man was saving himself for marriage, which was commendable but not Sam's thing. Life was too short to waste on rules that denied him happiness and pleasure. How that man ended up working in theater was beyond him, but there were odd birds everywhere.

Leuker lowered his body into a split with such ease Sam nearly groaned with excitement. How could he do that without straining a muscle? Leuker made it look so easy. Sam knew if he attempted such a move, he'd need a lift just to get himself standing upright again.

Sam watched the tension in Leuker's legs as his muscles throbbed the longer he held the position. He didn't look like he was in pain. Far from it. Euphoria rested on his face like sunlight on a warm beach. The longer he held that position, the more intense the curve of his leg muscles became. His buttocks flexed as he balanced himself. Watching Leuker made Sam's groin ache in a very pleasant way. If he could do that on stage, what could he do in bed?

He was certain Grant would be game, since Leuker looked so much like him and Sam was a great judge of character. The pseudo-identical-twin thing could be a bit disconcerting, but it also had to be very intriguing.

As much as I'd like to, I can't drool over him all day. I'll never get any work done.

Sam concentrated on tightening and positioning the row of lamps. The topmost lamps adjusted in a snap. He aimed them at the stage and pulled out the shutters. He'd worry about the colorful gels later. Once the gels were in place the stage would light up with beautiful hues, enhancing the dancers' movements in shadow and vibrant color. After one especially stubborn lamp refused to budge into its proper position without a near body slam, Sam stepped down from his ladder and collided with Leuker.

Sam caught the dancer in his arms before he could fall. "I'm sorry. Are you all right?"

His body rippled like running water in Sam's hands. Leuker, smaller and more sinewy than Grant, felt like a bundle of erotic tension ready to snap. Sam tried to resist caressing him, but his palms ran across Leuker's broad chest. An overwhelming urge to brush his hands against Leuker's narrow hips nearly overwhelmed Sam. He pulled away before his hands took on his wishes with a mind of their own.

"I'm okay, but you stepped on my foot." A rosy flush

flowed from his hairy chest to burn his cheeks.

How sweet. He's blushing.

A delightful giggle burst from his full lips. He looked down, averting his eyes from Sam's gaze, but those long, black lashes couldn't hide the green fire that burned in those irises. A shy smile spread across his face, bringing forth the most adorable dimples that matched Grant's.

My God, he looks so much like Grant I want to take him in my arms and ravish him.

Taking a chance, because he wanted so badly to touch the elegant dancer without a fall for an excuse, Sam rested one palm on Leuker's shoulder. At his touch, Leuker raised his head and stared into Sam's eyes. Sparks of interest shot from his gaze, and Sam felt the attraction all the way down to his groin. When Leuker's lips curled into a shy smile, Sam's heart ached with affection.

I'd better be careful. This one could easily get under my skin in a hurry. He's probably only in the group for this stop of the tour. I'll never see him again. Don't fall for him. Just enjoy him while you have the chance.

A wave of sadness washed over him. While he enjoyed traveling the country, he'd fantasized over the past month or two about staying put throughout the seasons. What would it be like to establish a long-term relationship with someone like Leuker, especially with Grant along for the ride? Charlotte and Lina excited his passions, as they did Grant's, but when it came to men in the company, no one had sparked as much interest as this delicious but shy dancer.

"I'm sorry I stepped on your foot. I'm Sam Hightower, gaffer. It's good to meet you. I didn't hurt you, did I?" Sam hitched in his breath when Leuker squeezed his bicep. It took all his will not to sweep the man up in his arms and plant a passionate kiss on his soft, sweet lips.

"No, you didn't hurt me." Leuker's honeyed voice broke Sam out of his distraction. "I'm Leuker Pearce, lead dancer.

Please call me Luke. You been with the troupe long?"

"Yes, since day one. You're new, right? I can't place your accent."

"I just came on board. I'm from Virginia. Norfolk."

His southern accent made the word Norfolk sound like "no fuck", which was the complete opposite of what Sam wanted to do.

"How are you liking Portland?" Sam asked.

"Oregon's nice. It's not nearly as hot and humid here as it is in Virginia. I'll be here for only about three days, though, then I move on to Seattle."

And out of my life forever once this stop ends. Think fast, man. I must find a way to get closer to him. Grant will want in on the action, too. I'm thinking for two people here.

Enamored of his shyness, Sam blocked Luke's path before he could leave. Luke brushed his fingers against Sam's shoulder like a caress. Although Sam resisted moaning with aroused joy, he gasped so loudly Luke noticed and smiled. Sam admired the strong arm and noticed the circular tattoo on his bicep. It looked like a snake eating its own tail.

"What kind of tattoo is that? I've seen it before, but I have no idea what it's called."

"It's an Ouroboros, a Greek symbol. It means constantly reforming oneself."

"Fascinating. I like it." Sam had often contemplated getting a tat, but he had no idea what kind to get. An Ouroboros would suit him perfectly, since as a shifter he constantly reformed himself. The endless changes exhausted him, but he couldn't avoid them.

"I hate to be rude, but I have to get back to practice, or I'll cramp."

Sam would have loved to take care of that cramp, but he kept his big mouth shut. Despite stifling his speech, his face must have been wide open, revealing the thoughts racing through his fevered mind. Luke cocked his head to one side and glanced at Sam with a faint smile and laughing eyes.

Good God, I'm a goner. This guy is getting to me.

They parted ways and went back to work.

Time passed quickly as Sam climbed ladders and hoisted lamps onto rigging paired with Grant. The two men laughed and touched as one held a lamp aloft whilst the other used a ratcheting wrench to screw it in place. Most of the lighting had been completed hours earlier. Now, the crew needed to aim the lights and adjust the shutters to the correct width, and the only way to do that properly was with the dancers present. Sam stole glances at Luke as he flowed across the stage.

Luke raised his head to give Sam a warm, shy smile, softening Sam's heart into a gooey lump in his chest.

Too late. I'm done for. He's under my skin. Am I sexy enough for him?

The dry air in the theater sent static through his hair. When he ran his hands over his tresses, he heard the crackles. As Sam's gaze traveled from Grant's wide shoulders to Luke's leaping form, he admired the softening of the edges his dancing gave his body. Yet, whilst much the same, the two men couldn't be any more different.

Grant's gruff nature was offset by Luke's warmth. Of course, Sam didn't know Luke at all, but he had his first impressions. Their brief meeting had brought the dancer's pleasant personality to light. He imagined hanging out with Luke, him drinking a stout and Luke drinking an IPA. Luke seemed to be the type to prefer his beer heavy on the hops. Assuming he drank beer. Did Luke like science fiction movies? Did he like cats? He wondered if Luke could cook, and if he did, what did he cook? Would he make a meal for Grant and him if they invited him over? Would they forgo eating altogether and make a meal out of each other?

Clearly shy and quiet, Luke took his time feeling Sam out, so different from Grant, who had barreled in when he and

Sam first met. Sam enjoyed Grant's aggressive attentions, which he displayed to this day, but he suspected Luke, with his blushing, didn't come on in such a bold and obvious manner. He seemed to be subtle to the point that Sam would have to ask directly what was on his mind.

During a break, Sam walked to the craft table to get a cup of coffee. He downed the brew along with a brownie the size of a brick to keep his strength up. God, what would he do when the world ran out of its cocoa supply? When he worked, he craved chocolate, and a brownie hit the spot.

Fingers tapped his shoulder. He turned to find Luke smiling at him, pouring a cup of coffee. Sam nearly fell over with shock and delight.

"You work hard out there, more than most of those other yahoos."

Excitement flowed through Sam's veins. "You've been watching me?"

"How could I not?" Luke cocked his head to the side and gave Sam another sweet, shy smile. "You're very attractive."

I'm a goner. "Thank you. You're pretty awesome yourself. You're a beautiful dancer."

"Thank you." He sipped his coffee.

Say something. Anything. Don't clam up now. "How long you been dancing?" *Oh, God, how lame was that? Could I come up with a better conversation starter?*

"About twenty years. I've been dancing since I was four."

"That's a long time. When I was four, I was still eating dirt in my back yard."

Luke laughed a hearty sound that rang in Sam's ears like bells. "I did my share of dirt eating, but I did it in ballet slippers." He touched Sam on the shoulder again, and Sam's heart skipped a few beats. "You work hard out there. I really appreciate it. I don't think the crew gets enough credit when it comes to shows like this one. It's heavy on the lighting. You're doing a great job."

Warmth crept up Sam's cheeks. He was sure his face was cherry red. Such commentary would have sounded insincere from many people in the theater, but Luke's sweetness and that delicious Virginia accent made him sound like he couldn't tell a lie even if he tried.

"Thank you," Sam said with a smile. "I do my best. So do the rest of the gaffers."

Luke cocked his head to one side and paused as if carefully considering what he was about to say. "You want to get together sometime, maybe go out for a beer?" he asked, his voice hesitant.

He's making it so easy for me to seduce him when the time is right

Sam's heart raced with excitement. Had Luke read his mind? Plus, Sam knew *"get together sometime"* was theater parlance for *"fuck like rabbits"*. He overheard Luke mention in passing his favorite beer was summer ale. Time to buy a case and put it in the fridge. What kind of music did he like? Something fast, hot and sexy, or gentle and romantic? Sam wanted an evening with Luke to fall into Barry White territory. Only the best nibbles for his shiny new lover. Or a complete meal? He had no idea. Grant would know better. He would just love him, especially since they looked so much alike.

"How about you come to my place after rehearsal tomorrow?" Sam asked. "You have to meet my partner, Grant Newsome. You and he bear a striking resemblance to each other." He grinned. "We'll have summer ale chilling in the fridge for you."

"That's my favorite kind of beer. How'd you know?" Luke gave him a sly smile, then that delightful laugh fell from those soft lips. "I'm game. How about midnight? We should be done by then."

"You're on."

"And I know I look like Grant. Hard to miss. Everyone's been pointing him out to me all day." His smile lit up his face. "But I had my eye on you."

Oh my God! He chose me! He noticed me! I feel like Sally Field at the Oscars!

The blush that flowed up Luke's cheeks delighted Sam. He wanted to respond, to tell Luke he'd noticed him, too. Hell, he wanted to sweep him up in his arms, but he didn't get the chance. The dancer seemed shy and dashed to the opposite wing.

Sam's mind raced with plans for the forthcoming night. He had only a few bottles of stout beer in the fridge. One case of summer ale should cover their date. Was it a date? Yes, it was! He needed to have snacks on hand. What went well with beer? He could pop popcorn but that would take too long. He and Grant would have time to stop at the grocery store before heading home. They'd probably pick up chips, chocolate, and nuts, the old reliables. Once he and Grant plied Luke with food and drink, they'd seduce him something fierce. Good thing Luke wasn't coming over until tomorrow. That would give them time to clean the dump.

Since they weren't home often, they tended to be a bit sloppy, although Grant was a true slob. Sam was considerably neater, but he wasn't fastidious or—God forbid—OCD. He didn't demand the towels line up evenly on the rack or keep the dishes color-coded. If he had, he wouldn't blame Grant for grumbling more than he already did about Sam reminding him to pick up his clothes from the floor or to put the toilet seat down.

Sam caught Grant's eye as Grant raced toward him.

"I see you two are hitting it off. Are we going to have a guest soon?"

"Yup. I invited him to our place tomorrow night. He's coming over after rehearsal around midnight."

Grant smiled. "Beer and snacks afterwards?"

"One can wish." Sam squeezed Grant's bicep. "I hope that's all right."

"Are you kidding? I always wanted to masturbate in the

third person."

Love surged in Sam's breast at his admiration of Grant's sense of humor. "We'll have a grand old-time tomorrow night, just the three of us."

"Looking forward to it."

Sam looked around but saw no sign of Luke. Disappointed, he poured himself a second cup of coffee, drank it, and went back to work.

CHAPTER TWO

Blocking (n): positioning and movement of actors on a stage in preparation for a performance.
Block (v): cock blocking — a person who prevents another man from scoring sexually.

The crowd at the Black Horse Pub was hopping that night. The main bar comprised the first room. Men dressed in bright orange vests and thick plaid shirts filled the tables and the chairs at the wraparound bar. Some in their early twenties wearing slim jeans and ski sweaters sat in tables near the windows overlooking the woods. Somehow, the guys playing two guitars and a set of drums were able to fit in a tight corner. The lighting sucked, but Sam wasn't there to light up the band, which played top '70s rock and roll hits. Typical bar fare.

Wood paneling and stained oak beams on the ceiling comprised the middle room. A fire roared in a brick fireplace in the center of the wall. A woman dressed in an oversized black sweater and slim black jeans sat in an overstuffed armchair in front of the fire, reading a book. A glass of chardonnay sat on a small table to her right. She had removed her sensible shoes and rested her stockinged feet on the antique oriental rug that filled the expanse of the floor. Two more chairs faced the fire, but they sat empty. Sam wondered how that woman could read with all the noise surrounding her.

Three dart boards hung on the walls in the third room. Five

hunters stood in the room trying to outdo each other's rankings and failing miserably with each swig of beer they drank. There were no TVs in this bar. It was not a sports bar. It was a hunter's bar, where the men came after a day of shooting and missing the multitude of deer that lived in the surrounding woods. When one got lucky and shot a ten-point buck, they drank. When one was unfortunate enough to miss that same ten-point buck, they drank. It could be a rough crowd at times, with the drinking and the noise. Sometimes fights broke out, but they ended as quickly as they began.

At Charlotte's urging, Sam ordered a pitcher of beer for the table. Everyone pitched in, as they did with every pitcher. While this was a hunter's bar, anyone was welcome, including the theater people. Being a cold autumn night, stout beer would hit the spot. Sam agreed, especially since Charlotte was rarely wrong.

"It's really busy tonight," Lina said. "Any reason in particular?"

"I have no idea," Grant said. He rarely paid attention to the goings-on about town.

"It's not a holiday yet," Sam said. "Halloween isn't for a few more weeks. Maybe the drunks have nowhere else to hang out."

Charlotte punched him on the arm, making him squeal in mock pain. "Drunks gotta have their own place, too, ya know. Hey, look, there's Luke. Make room." She waved her arms over her head as if guiding a plane onto a tarmac. When Luke saw her, he smiled and made his way to the table.

Grant grabbed a chair from a table next to them and placed it next to him. As Luke sat down, Charlotte placed a pint glass in front of him.

"I hope you like stout. It's what's for dinner," she said.

"I love it. Steak and stout pie is one of my favorite dishes. I make it on occasion," he said.

"Not only can he dance, he can cook," Charlotte said as she poured him some stout. "Good thing you're AC-DC. We can make beautiful music together. After we eat, of course."

"Charlotte, you're far too tempting to resist," Luke said. "I've never met anyone with as much . . .enthusiasm as you have."

"That's a kind way of putting it." Lina said with a giggle.

"Sweetness, you have a beer foam mustache. Let me lick it off." Charlotte leaned over and flicked her pointed tongue across Lina's upper lip, taking the foam with it.

The two women kissed with such quick, heated passion a few guys at the bar couldn't help but stop to look. Sam fought back a snicker as the horny bunch licked their own lips, clearly wishing they could get in on the action. Fat chance of that happening. Charlotte and Lina chose their lovers on each leg of the tour with great care. Those rednecks could only dream of bedding them. Charlotte especially liked to flaunt her luscious looks and sexuality in public where she was most likely to get a rise out of the men watching, in every sense of the word rise. Despite their pickiness, they did like their bedpost notches.

If a man—or woman—had an especially alluring look or a fascinating personality, the two women were likely to have their way with them. Most people who made it onto their radar didn't stand a chance of resisting. That was' how irresistible Charlotte and Lina were. Sam was glad he and Grant were in their inner circle. They were friends as well as lovers, something that Charlotte and Lina did not often allow.

"Stop showing off, you two," Sam said. "You're attracting a crowd."

Charlotte pulled away from Lina and blew a kiss at him. Always the fun-lover, she kept the men at the table on their toes. She did the same thing with every man in the bar. If only they knew how much more she enjoyed women than they did.

"A riled-up crowd at that." Grant said, turning to Luke. "Any idea why there are so many people here tonight?"

"I heard there's going to be some kind of redneck town meeting. Something big is going down," Luke said.

"A redneck town meeting?" Grant asked. "I wonder what on earth that could be about? Beer, hunting, and reality TV?"

Charlotte tapped Grant and Luke on the backs of their hands. "Do you two have any idea how much staring at you is like looking at a fun house mirror?"

"Yes," they said in unison and laughed.

Sam often wondered about their doubling appearance. Would Luke be as rough as Grant could be in bed? Looking at the buff dancer who sipped his drink with a delicate touch, he doubted it. Luke would serenade his body while Grant roughhoused with it. He was eager to find out exactly how, and he would learn soon enough.

Thinking about sex with his two look-alikes made his other appetite appear with a vengeance. Working always made him fantasize about cheese fries, potato skins, and the Black Horse's patented cream of crab soup with a dash of sherry. He waved over a frazzled waitress who took everyone's order. Cream of crab soup and steak tips for Sam. Rare. Baked potato on the side. Grant ordered the hot and sour soup and nachos. Luke ordered a salad. The girls usually ordered the same thing as each other, and this evening was no different. Tonight, it was the veal parmesan with fresh green beans on the side, plain for Lina and covered with pepper for Charlotte.

"Do you want a little veal with your pepper?" Sam loved teasing Charlotte. She was a good sport about it, too. She would get her revenge, though. Charlotte loved nothing better than a good practical joke.

"You're bad, you know that?" she said.

"Of course. You wouldn't have me any other way."

She laughed and sipped her stout, crossing her eyes at him.

"What are you ordering, Luke?" Sam asked.

"Mesclun greens salad with caramelized walnuts and a big bowl of vegetarian chili."

"Oh, yeah," Grant said. "Luke doesn't like real food."

"I don't eat meat. I don't like the idea of eating food someone had to chase down."

Sam nearly choked on his stout. Luke had no idea how right he was.

After their food arrived, Sam didn't bother to wait out of politeness. He was so famished he dug right in.

"How's the cow?" Luke asked.

"Fantastic. Nice and tender." Sam grinned as he stuffed a nice forkful in his mouth. He closed his eyes and chewed, making his feasting a big production for Luke. "Bloody as hell, too, just the way I like it."

"I don't see how you can eat that. Do you have any idea how many hormones that dead beast has been injected with?

"Do you know how much pesticide has been sprayed on that grass you're grazing on?" Sam teased. "Be careful. Your balls could be shrinking as we speak."

"My balls only shrink right before I come."

Sam nearly choked on his steak. Grant let out a big belly laugh.

"You could ask us about all that, but we'd keep our big mouths shut," Charlotte said.

It was Lina's turn to laugh. "I can't imagine you, the Gossip Queen, keeping her mouth shut about anything, even though you do keep a secret." She turned to Sam. "She has a mouth like a steel trap. I've never met anyone who loves to keep a secret the way she does."

"How can she keep a secret and be a Gossip Queen at the same time?" Sam asked.

"You'd be surprised. She only gossips about what is

common knowledge, but she knows everyone secrets long before word gets out."

She doesn't know my secret. Or Grant's.

"She'd be a good buddy to have in your corner, then. I'm glad she likes us. I don't want to think about what ammo she has on us."

"I have some pretty good ammo," Charlotte said, "but I don't kiss and tell."

"No, she doesn't," Luke said.

"You know this how?" Grant asked.

"He's not the only one who's heteroflexible," Charlotte said.

"Heteroflexible?" Grant's eyebrows shot up. "I like that one. I'll have to use it in a full sentence sometime soon."

"You've never heard that word before?" Lina said. "You're out of touch."

"Call me naïve," Grant said. "I don't keep up with things. You will have to teach me how you two are heteroflexible."

"Oh, happily," Lina said.

"Whoa, quiet down. It looks like something's going on over there." Sam nodded in the direction of the front of the pub.

One rather rotund man wearing stained jeans and a checked flannel shirt that barely covered his beer gut waved the rowdy crowd into silence by tapping a pint glass with a spoon. Once the crowd quieted down, he spoke. What he had to say chilled Sam to his core.

"Everyone should be loaded up with enough ammo by now. You know the rules. Shoot to kill. We've had enough problems losing livestock to disease this season. The last thing we need is wolves attacking. We have to stop them before they attack again."

Did these clowns have any idea two werewolves lived in their vicinity? Sam looked out the window at the glow of the rising full moon hidden behind clouds. He and Grant would need to shift and run to get the blood fire out of their systems after they left the Black Horse, but they did not want to run into any of these people. The crowd of men hummed with chatter as they ordered more beer.

The last thing Sam wanted was to run into drunken rednecks brandishing rifles while he ran on all fours in the woods. He recognized Beer Belly. The man was a fixture in the bar. Did he even have a job? What did his wife and kids do while he spent all the money on booze and fantasy football bets? Did he even have a wife and kids? Most likely, he did. That sort always did. A run-in with any of these clowns meant certain death or serious injury at the very least. He leaned toward Grant and whispered quietly enough for his lover to hear but not for anyone else at the table to catch his words.

"Is it legal to hunt wolves here?"

"No, but this situation seems different, since wolves are destroying livestock and harming people." Grant whispered.

"What are we going to do?"

"Don't worry." Grant whispered. "I know the area better than you do. We'll be fine. They're expecting ordinary wolves, not anything like us."

Several men stood, carrying rifles. A few even had crossbows. Nothing hurt worse than a crossbow bolt. Pulling the thing out only made the injury worse, but running with a bolt in your hide wasn't much better. How safe could he and Grant possibly be with this crowd on the loose? Plenty of wolves lurked in the area, hunting by night with so much stealth Sam didn't see them. He could smell them, though, especially when he fully or partially shifted. As far as he knew, wolves attacked only wildlife, rabbits, deer, an occasional 'possum. They sometimes homed in on a raccoon, but those things were so vicious they mostly avoided them. If the locals were right that the wolves were attacking livestock, that was a serious problem.

They needed to be careful for the next few nights when he and Grant ran through the woods, venting their frustrations under the light of the full moon. Once the moon phase changed, they'd have another twenty-eight days of peace until the next full moon. The cycle never ended, although Sam often wished it would. He loved Grant and couldn't be with him any other way, but the endless moon cycles wore him out. He kept a calendar app on his phone for that very reason. Now he had to add hungry hunters and drunks to his list of troubles vexing him.

A handful of men left the pub. To Sam's relief, most stayed behind to finish their pints. At least the alcohol would deaden their senses and cause their aim to go wobbly. Never before had Sam been happy to see a group of drunks get totally inebriated. As long as they kept drinking, they were both unlikely to see them, and if they did, their aim would be so bad they'd hit everything but him and Grant.

By the time the last pitcher was gone, it was nearly two. A fire burned in Sam, wanting release. He looked at Grant, and by his expression, he knew Grant wanted the same thing. They excused themselves, wished everyone well for the night, and left the pub.

CHAPTER THREE

Whip (v): To apply whipping twine to the ends of a rope to prevent it unraveling—In rigging, a whip is a single line over a single sheave used to aid handling.
Whip (n): A popular bondage device made of leather and other materials to inflict pain.

Grant choked down several swallows of his monkshood rye concoction, hoping it would make his transformation less painful and intense. He'd drank this fetid swill for many years. Time had not improved the taste. The thick fluid stuck to the roof of his mouth, and it tasted of gravel. Rye, a grain with a sharp, sour, and tangy taste, made Grant's eyes water. Monkshood, otherwise known as wolfsbane, was an herb long known for keeping Lycans at bay. It also kept the shifting at bay so he wouldn't go full werewolf, and rye dulled the graveyard dirt taste. Despite the lovely purple flowers, the herb poisoned anyone who ingested it, leaving an intense burning sensation in the limbs and stomach in its wake. Large doses could kill in only a couple of hours, but in small amounts, it prevented him and Sam from completely shifting. Plus, the alcohol gave him a bit of an edge. It also made him tipsy if he drank enough of it. It was a good thing he didn't have to work in the morning. While the concoction didn't prevent him from turning, it took some of the agony out of it.

He thought back to his fateful trip to Germany, when he was an ordinary human being. What would it be like to enjoy a night out on the town drinking and carousing by the light of the full moon like he had in Freiberg, the night his life had changed forever?

What if he hadn't gone hiking that night? What if he'd stayed in the Stag's Head Inn instead, enjoying pint after pint of pilsner? In many ways, the Black Horse reminded him of the Stag's Head. Both were small, rather claustrophobic dives sporting deer heads on the walls. Peanut shells covered the sticky floors. Beer flowed freely.

What if things had been different? even the smallest change could have affected his future. His buddy Heinrich was fifteen minutes late getting to the Stag's Head, just in time to miss seeing Grant getting up to leave. Had he arrived on time he would have convinced Grant to stay for a few more hours rather than go for a short walk in the Black Forest where Grant had run into the beast.

Although he had been warned to avoid the short cut through the forest to get to the hostel, he was tired and a bit too drunk to think clearly. The thick woods hid all manner of secrets, and the lonely road beckoned. The full moon lighting his way gave him a deceptive air of invulnerability. Who would attack him in the dead of night on a lonely road into Freiberg? Thieves? He shook his head at the warnings the locals gave, telling him of beasts that prowled the roads in the dead of night. Such silliness, local superstitions.

One local in particular at the inn had been especially aggressive toward him, but he put it to the guy drinking far too much bourbon. He wondered if homophobia had clouded the man's rage, but he put that miserable thought out of his mind. Mr. Drunk-on-Bourbon lost a billiards match to Grant, and he did not like parting with his wallet. Grant recalled his sour mash breath tinged with the scent of the smoked sausage he had eaten. The man's bloodshot rheumy blue-eyed gaze bore into Grant, making him feel very uncomfortable. He wanted to put as much distance as possible between that drunk and himself. By one-thirty, tired and feeling a bit woozy from drink, he left the inn, ignoring the man's warning to take the main road even though it added ten minutes to his walk.

He was well into the Black Forest when the howling began. Suddenly sober with fright, he raced down the moonlit path as quickly as he could, seeing the hostel not far in the distance, but he wasn't fast enough. The howling circled him, finally emerging from his left. The beast that jumped him shoved him to the ground so roughly it knocked the wind out of him. One huge paw swiped sharp claws into his shoulder, and he cried out in pain. He looked into the beast's face and smelled sour mash and smoked sausage on its breath. The rheumy blue, bloodshot eyes that bored into him looked human.

"I told you to avoid the forest, you cocky bastard." The beast growled. "Now you'll get what's coming to you."

Teeth gored his wounded shoulder. The harder Grant shoved, the stronger the beast's grip became. Within moments gunshots rang out. Welcome yelps and whooping greeted him as the townsfolk from the inn raced toward them, but the bullets they fired only flew above the beast's head. It released its grip, glared at Grant, spat in his face, and fled into the underbrush.

The townsfolk helped Grant to his feet, but he shoved them off, stumbling toward the hostel where he cleaned and dressed his wound, which looked much worse than it felt. He left Freiberg for the States the next day, trying to put his ordeal out of his mind, but he couldn't ignore his terror of what he knew he would become at the next full moon.

He shifted one month later, alone and terrified while he swam in a lake away from prying eyes. He'd known he would change, so he'd avoided crowds. When his torso and limbs first elongated, the pain was so intense he nearly drowned. He screamed in agony, but his guttural shout turned into a wolfen howl that he quickly quieted. He watched in horror as his hands lengthened, hair coarsening, and fingernails turning into claws. His internal organs shifted, giving him incredible pain. Scared out of his wits, he hid in the water until dawn after he shifted back into his human form. He had no frame of reference, no Lycan mentor. He didn't even know if such a thing existed.

Fearful of everyone around him since he was so different, he trusted no one. Being attracted to both men and women in 1931 was hard enough without keeping his status as a shifter hidden from prying eyes. Forever a strapping young man, Grant often worked house construction, not exactly the most forgiving job when it came to flirting with muscle-bound men.

Oh, he took lovers here and there, a man he met on a bridge project, another youth he picked up in a bar, and many others. He couldn't allow those relationships to continue lest his lovers discover his secret. He couldn't risk his life for someone he didn't care that much about for many reasons, the most obvious one being the danger each month from shifting into his wolf form. He refused to allow any man—or woman for that matter—to get close enough to him to learn his true nature.

The other problem was explaining how his lovers would age if they remained together for any lengthy period of time. He stayed as youthful as ever without a portrait of himself aging in an attic while he remained young in the world like the fictional character.

He remained alone for four decades until he met Sam. A big reason he held onto Sam was that Sam had accidentally discovered his secret. In July of 1969, shortly before Woodstock during the Summer of Love, Grant dropped and broke his bottle of monkshood rye and nearly completely shifted in front of Sam because he didn't have enough booze to prevent the change. Sam panicked, of course. Any man would in his position. He attacked Grant with anything he could find. Including a Louisville slugger, a metal chair, and last, a hunky, male celebrity body pillow a friend had made for him. That last one amused Grant so much he laughed and stopped shifting. The sight of a werewolf snickering so heartily with drool running down his snout shocked Sam to the point he was overcome with uncomfortable but amused laughter. Luckily, Grant had eaten deer earlier that evening and did not turn Sam into a tasty meal.

For once, Grant found a man he could share his most intimate secrets with. He told Sam the whole story about Freiberg. Sam asked how he could break the curse, and Grant honestly didn't know. He'd heard rumors saying he needed to find the werewolf who'd turned him and kill it, but silver bullets were a myth. Werewolves could be felled like any other animal, but their hides were especially tough, so ammo didn't penetrate as easily as it would for, say, a buck or a buffalo. As Grant became more comfortable in Sam's presence, he exposed his feelings like a flower opening its petals to the sun. Trust did not come easily to Grant, but as he learned to trust that Sam would not hurt him in any way, his attachment to his new lover grew stronger. As the two of them opened to each other, their infatuation and fascination grew into love.

They offset each other perfectly. Grant was a bit of a slob. Not to the point of being a health hazard, but enough to annoy Sam, who constantly ribbed him over his untidiness. In his effort to please his lover, Grant remembered to pick up his dirty socks and to make his side of the bed every morning. Both men could cook and enjoyed a hearty homemade meal when they could get it. Life on the road didn't always afford anything other than roadie grub, which was passable but nothing like a home-cooked beef roast with potatoes, peas, and carrots. Grant was definitely a meat and potatoes lover.

Sam teased him about how he could eat his pick of fresh animals when they hunted in the woods on the full moon. Although he was also a devoted carnivore, Sam occasionally liked vegetarian lasagna and Caesar salads overflowing with croutons.

By the time crocuses peeked through the snow in 1970, they were a very serious item, so serious Sam begged Grant to turn him. This was not an idle request. They had long discussed how Sam's life would become secretive, nomadic, and he would become a slave to the moon phases if Grant did what he wanted. Nothing could deter Sam. He was in love, and that was all there was to it. Grant had fallen hard, too. He wasn't immune to Sam's delightful sense of humor and his way of pulling Grant out of a depressed funk. Grant couldn't help but laugh when Sam rang out in his cheer to bring up Grant's piss poor mood. He'd sing out the letters of his name while giving arm movements to mimic the letters. *Gimme a G! Gimme an R! Gimme an A!* By the time Sam made it to the letter N, Grant always doubled over with laughter.

Grant remembered the day he chose Sam as his shifting partner as if it were yesterday. On April 21, 1970, he bit into Sam's hip as they made love. His bite was deep enough to draw blood. Sam shifted later that month, but unlike Grant, he had a mentor to guide him through the confusion and terror. Hidden by dark skies and underbrush, he and Grant had hunted for the first time together.

After many decades, Grant had grown weary of running and hiding, and that evening drove his melancholia home harder than ever.

There he sat with Sam in the Portland forest, part human and part wolf, smoking and drinking, waiting for their meal to appear. Grant sat in front of Sam while Sam rubbed his shoulders.

So much had changed over time. Now, he relied on his iPhone to keep track of moon phases. Before his trip to Freiberg, he hadn't even noticed the moon in the sky at all. No matter where he lived or toured, he had taken to hiding out in the nearest forest on those couple of nights each month when the blood lust took over his mind and body. No one was safe when he transformed, and he did what he could to avoid harming people. A deer or stray dog quenched his blood lust while he hid from the world in the safety of the deepest area of the forest, waiting until the full moon decayed the five percent he needed to be out of trouble. He only transformed at night, and his gallon jug of monkshood rye alleviated his symptoms somewhat, but in the end, he knew he was a danger and needed to hide, not only to avoid killing people but to keep away from the local authorities.

He crouched on the forest floor, swatting the black flies that bit through his thick fur. He wished there were some way of reversing the curse thrust upon him. He wanted nothing more than to sit at home with Sam, drink some beer, and watch a porn flick while making love to Sam again. He cursed his bad timing and rotten luck. He could say *"if only"* until the tides reversed. Nothing would change the fact that he would go feral every full moon. While he accepted his fate, he did not like it at all. Each full moon he fell into a rage that often came with thoughts of suicide, but when he thought of Sam and his sweet nature and even sweeter body, he realized he had reason to stay alive.

Sam sat next to him, smoking a cigarette, and Grant handed him the jug. Why did Sam seem to take to the change better than he? Or did he really take to it better? What if Sam only pretended so that Grant wouldn't feel so bad? Misery loved company, but Sam, being a good-natured sort, didn't wallow in sorrow. He considered the moonlit change a monthly inconvenience, much like some women considered their menstrual cycles. An irritant. If only Grant felt the same way.

Sam gulped as he drank, making slurping noises that grated in Grant's ears. Sometimes Grant considered the potion the only control he had over his life.

"I feel miserable. I hate the full moon," Grant said. "Sometimes I just want to curl up and die."

"It will last only another day or two and then things will be back to normal."

"What kind of normal is this kind of life?" Grant let his chin rest on his chest as Sam rubbed the kinks out of his shoulders. "My entire body hurts. The monkshood rye helps, but I'm as sore as I know I'll be every month."

"I know what you mean. We need something strong for the pain, like morphine, but I don't know where to get it."

"I'd rather have cyanide."

"Don't talk like that. We can get through this."

Grant groaned in ecstasy as Sam's fingers rubbed down his spine. Even though his entire body ached and he wanted to do nothing more than sleep for the next two days, his cock reacted to Sam's amorous touch, growing larger and becoming sensitive to the slightest touch.

"Hey, I found a great movie for us to watch," Sam said. "*The Brotherhood of the Wolf*. I figured it was the perfect movie for our time of the month."

"Never heard of it."

Sam turned to Grant and gave him a look Grant was all too familiar with. It was the *you've got to be shitting me* look, since Sam enjoyed relishing in the ways of the world much more than Grant.

"You can't be serious. What kind of werewolf are you when you've never heard of *The Brotherhood of the Wolf?*"

"I just don't get into those kinds of movies. I like action

movies. You know that."

"Tell you what. I'll bring it home in a day or two, and we'll watch it. It's really good, and it won't gross you out." He grinned. "It's French, too."

"That means it has subtitles. I hate reading subtitles. No thanks, I'll pass."

"How about *An American Werewolf in London*?"

"I told you, no werewolf movies. I'd rather watch *Lock, Stock, and Two Smoking Barrels* again."

"How about *The Transporter Two*? I hear it's so bad it's good. What about that one?"

Grant shuffled on the ground, picked up the jug of monks-hood rye, and gulped some down. Pointedly ignoring Sam, he gazed into the forest, hoping something big and tasty would come out soon. Maybe a deer if they got lucky. He was famished, and he wanted to eat rather than waste time and energy talking about movies he didn't like.

"C'mon, what do you say? It's got Jason Statham in it. You like him."

"Okay, that sounds good. Just no werewolf movies, please. What got into you to watch werewolf movies when the moon is full? That's like watching *Rosemary's Baby* when you're pregnant."

"I like to have fun with it, rather than mope about like you. You wallow in it. My first werewolf, and you turn out to be overly sensitive."

"Oh, knock it off." His sensitive ears picked up rustling in the brush several yards ahead. "Now shush. I hear food in the bushes. Shh."

A 'possum emerged from the brush, oblivious to the danger that lurked only a few yards away. Grant had not tasted 'possum in several months, and he welcomed the change. He needed to eat meat when he shifted, but he didn't want to call attention to himself by eating his neighbor's pets or any

animals that would be missed. That left the usual gopher, raccoon, or rat if they missed getting anything in the woods.

What I would do for some fresh venison, though.

He eyed up the unsuspecting creature's flesh, salivating so
much he could almost taste its meat, red and bloody, raw and
metallic. Inching in, ever so slowly, so as to not so much as
break a twig, he crept towards the 'possum, and when he was
ready to pounce, he heard a loud ka-boom from behind.

The 'possum shrieked and fled into the forest. Birds flew
from the trees. Furious, Grant turned on his heels and
growled at Sam.

"Dammit, Sam, you sneezed, and that 'possum got away
from me."

"I couldn't help it. Allergies. I took Claritin early evening
before we changed, but I guess I need a prescription."

"Ya think? If you sneeze again and drive away a perfectly
good meal, I might have to disembowel you myself."

"C'mon, I said I was sorry. Lie back and I'll make it up to
you."

Grant stretched out on the grass, arms behind his head and
legs extended, waiting for Sam's gentle touch. When Sam's
hand stroked his chest, his heart skipped a couple of beats.
Even Sam's slightest touch aroused him. His cock jumped a
little, in anticipation of what he knew was coming.

*The sex will take my mind off my hunger. There's nothing as dis-
tracting as a good blow job, especially from Sam.*

Grant relished Sam's exquisite blow jobs, and he knew Sam
would not disappoint him.

*I need him, need his touch on me, anything to take my mind off
this burning need for flesh.*

Sam's lips brushed Grant's shoulder, then traveled down
his chest to rest near his groin. Closing his eyes to fully enjoy
Sam's kiss, he waited for those soft lips to reach his cock.

Brushing against his head in tight, slow circles, Sam's lips
wrapped around Grant's cock, and in response Grant dug his

fingers into the earth. With a gentle movement, those lips and mouth stroked his shaft, making it jump in Sam's mouth.

No other man ever had this kind of effect on me. I can't resist the mere touch of him against me.

Sam's tongue, slick and warm, flicked in circles around Grant's shaft. His erection grew harder as Sam's tongue moved faster around him. Sam alternated between stroking Grant's shaft with his tongue, then sucking hard on his head, all the while rolling his balls in his hand.

Moaning with pleasure, Grant tensed as Sam took all of him deep into his mouth, sucking and licking, driving him wild. Grabbing Sam's head in his hands, he pushed him harder against his cock, taking in his entire length. The approaching orgasm made his heart race, but the sounds of motors interrupted his passion. Grant opened his eyes in time to see a shooting star skitter below the full moon.

Who is stupid enough to drive into the forest knowing there are wolves about? Little do they know what really lurks out here.

Two burly men on dirt bikes bounced into the forest clearing as Grant and Sam rushed to find cover behind a copse of maple trees. To Grant's horror, the two men stopped in the middle of the clearing. They stood less than thirty feet away. One grabbed a twelve pack of beer, and they stepped away from their bikes.

"Hey, Louis, toss me a brew. This driving about is making me thirsty."

Lewis tore open the twelve pack and threw a bottle at his friend. "You sure we should be out here? With the wolf warnings and all?"

"What are you, chicken shit? We ain't gonna see no wolves. Besides, I have my gun." He pulled a pistol from his back waistband and waved it in the air, setting off one round.

"Are you out of your mind, man? Don't go attracting attention to us out here."

Sam whispered, "Those two aren't going to go away any

time soon, are they?"

"No, and they smell like they've been drinking for hours. I can smell their sweat and stale booze breath from here."

Hackles stood up on his back as the two men guzzled their beer. The lust for blood and fresh kill overwhelmed him so much he scraped the ground with his razor-sharp claws.

"If we move quietly, we can get away without them seeing us. Be careful. They look trigger-happy to me," Grant said.

Grant crept through the brush, followed by a quivering Sam. Could they ease their way through the bushes without calling attention to themselves? Heart thudding hard, he crouched as low to the ground as he could, but he didn't take Sam's less careful pace into consideration. He knew Sam was more frightened than he, and that fear took its toll when Sam snapped a large branch in two when he put his weight on it. The two rednecks turned in the direction of the sound. Grant grabbed Sam's wrist and froze.

He and his lover stood as motionless as they could, but their best efforts were thwarted. Both men must have seen their shining yellow eyes and their massive height by the light of the full moon. They screamed.

Grant's legs shivered with terror. *This is it. This is when we end up riddled with bullets. Don't move a muscle.*

The stink of piss rose on the breeze as the taller man backed away. He ran for his dirt bike to race away, and a cloud of dirt followed in his wake. Rising to face the other drunk who stood before them frozen in terror, Sam lunged and howled at the drunk and lashed at him with his sharp claws. The drunk broke free and fled to his bike.

"We sure blew it, didn't we?" Grant asked, watching the bike disappear in the distance. "Now what's going to happen to us? Those two are going to tell everyone what happened."

"Who's going to believe a couple of drunks? Yeah, they'll talk werewolf, and they'll be laughed out of the bar. No one will believe that, but they will believe they were attacked by wolves."

"We have to move. Once word gets out those two were at-tacked, they'll bring their drinking buddies out here, and we better be gone before that happens."

Sam patted Grant on the back. "Let's get out of here before the crowd comes calling."

They headed north, running farther into the forest, where brush and trees grew thickly along the quarry. Grant followed Sam into that direction. Soon gunshots roared and motors revved behind them. Frantic baying terrified Grant.

More bikers, with hounds no less, and they came from all directions. He panicked. How were they going to get away without getting killed? They needed to head for water to mask their scent so the hounds would not find them. The nearest water source was the quarry that was nearly three miles away.

Grant ran in a jagged path through the forest, hoping he was moving away from the drunks and their dogs. His heart trip-hammered in his chest, each thump shouting his fear of getting shot or worse. Sweat poured down his hairy brow, and his jaw locked with anxiety. He took a few deep breaths to keep from hyperventilating.

Sam followed not far behind, but he was not as fast on his feet, forcing Grant to slow his pace for Sam to be able to keep up. If only Sam ran faster.

Every full moon left Grant terrified, wondering if he'd get through the night alive. If only he could find the man who turned him and destroy him. Maybe that would end his curse.

Most of the howling and yelping came from behind, but Grant heard more calls ahead of him on the left and slightly behind on the right. He ran ahead of the noise, hoping they could maneuver through the forest before the mad crowd en-circled them.

Gunshots blasted less than fifty yards behind them. Sick to

his stomach, Grant ran faster. He feared he and Sam weren't going to make it. Were they going to die in a hail of bullets before they even reached the quarry? At this rate, if the drunks coming from ahead of them closed their ranks, they were goners.

All humanity left him as he raced for his life. His body shifted into full wolf mode, as did Sam's behind him. Fear always overcame the monkshood rye drink. Hell, this wasn't merely fear. It was stark raving terror. A bullet whizzed by his ear and slammed into a tree to his left. Drunks called from behind, coming closer.

"I see them, Ray. Two of 'em. Bigger than any wolves I've ever seen."

"Them ain't no wolves."

"Get 'em. Aim between the shoulder blades."

A bullet grazed Grant's left shoulder. He yelped in pain, but he did not slow his pace. Nerves alert, he agonized over the next bullet—would it strike him in the head? Sam ran at his side, panting in fear and exhaustion. Forward they pressed, faster and faster, until Grant's limbs ached. His muscles cramped so tightly he feared they'd seize, stopping him dead in his tracks. He couldn't afford to slow even a smidge. Terror pushed tears into his eyes. He was going to die out here in those woods, surrounded by drunken locals who had no idea what they were really dealing with.

After a twenty-minute run that seemed to last forever, the two reached the quarry. The water was so close, yet so far. Panic overwhelmed Grant, and he worried that this time he would finally be caught and killed. Imagine, killed by a group of drunken rednecks. That was not the way he wanted to die.

Worked up into a sweat, Grant craved a cool, refreshing dip. The water in the quarry was deep and cold, exactly what he needed. The cold water would chill his overheated body.

Hounds howled in the distance, following their scent. They somehow had to lose those mutts.

Once they reached the water's edge, they dived in. He and Sam swam to the opposite side of the quarry, far away from the madding crowd and their dogs, and rested in a copse of blackberry bushes.

Several minutes of panting exhaustion passed before either one spoke.

"How long do you think they'll hunt for us?" Sam asked.

"I don't know, but I hope they leave soon." Grant's body trembled from both fear and shock. Anger bubbled beneath the wide-ranging emotions. Anger over the creature that had turned him into this accursed fiend that emerged every full moon, and he knew there was nothing he could do to make his life any different. How he hated the way his body reacted to the full moon. His broad shoulders grew to monstrous proportions. His arms and legs were out of proportion to the rest of his body as they lengthened. When he crouched upright, he could drag his knuckles on the ground. He didn't like being a knuckle-dragger. He'd learned long ago to wear very loose and comfortable clothing when the moon was full.

In his early days, he lost plenty of good clothing to tears and seams ripping as his body grew. He especially resented losing an expensive silk shirt he had bought shortly after being changed. So much could go wrong when he shifted. He couldn't make plans. He couldn't be sure he'd live through the night when he hid in the forest no matter where he lived, and he had lived in many locations. Massachusetts, Maryland, Germany, France, Canada, and other lands he'd stayed in so briefly he couldn't remember them. Oh for the chance to settle down in one place and stop chasing their demons around the world. Sam didn't know Grant's wanderlust had faded after years of roaming. How would he tell him he wanted to settle in one place?

All he wanted to do was race home and curl up in his bed for the next few days until the full moon faded, but that was out of the question. If only he could return to Freiberg and change his destiny.

"We'd better get home before daylight," Sam said.

"I agree with you. I don't hear the drunks anymore. I think we're safe. Now let's get out of here."

"No, not yet. Let's wait a bit longer."

Eager to get home but not eager to run into more rednecks, they stayed put for what Grant estimated was another hour. Only when the sole sounds they heard were crickets chirping and night peepers singing in the grass did they rush through the forest, listening for the sound of the crowd gaining on them. The howls and yelling had disappeared.

Grant was grateful their home backed up to the woods and that the current spot in the tour was close enough that he and Sam didn't have to find temporary lodging. They didn't have to wander through town in the dead of night. While their townhouse was a small three stories, it was home. The living room faced the road. An eat-in kitchen faced their spacious backyard that backed up to the woods. There were no lights behind the homes save a porchlight here and there. They could safely rush through the woods in feral form and race to the back door without being seen. They kept the sliding screen back door unlocked on shifting nights. The neighborhood was so safe they could have left the door unlocked all the time, but after living years in big cities, neither of them felt comfortable doing that.

The master bedroom on the second floor faced the backyard, and a small nook with a daybed faced the road. The washer and dryer were in front of the master bath. Two guest rooms and a second, smaller bath were on the third floor. They used the rooms for storage and crash space for friends and crew members who needed to say overnight.

Grant liked the place so much he wanted to make it a permanent home. If only he were able to plant a garden in the backyard. He could grow his own monkshood and herbs for cooking like rosemary, thyme, and oregano. Sam, on the other hand, had a black thumb. The leaves fell off his plastic rubber plant every time he dusted it. Grant had never seen anyone else kill a fake shrub.

While the streets were mostly deserted, there were isolated pockets of people awake at this ungodly hour, like drunks leaving the bars for the night, workers coming off the midnight shift, hungry folk hanging out at Denny's at o-dark-thirty in the morning. They could not risk being seen, which meant being caught.

The full moon lit their way, and soon the forest thinned as they approached the edge. Following the familiar dirt path that led to the back of Elkhorn Cove where they lived, Grant passed the lake, the wooded dance pavilion, and the children's playground he knew were only a few hundred yards from his backyard.

Almost home . . . keep moving . . . not much farther.

Gritting his teeth, he resisted crying out or—worse yet—howling. No matter how much he wanted to let off the steam, he knew he couldn't utter a sound. Feeling lightheaded from excitement and shock, he charged forward, wishing he could stop to rest but knowing once he stopped, he would no longer have the energy to flee.

As he and Sam approached the clearing that led to their backyard, they slowed down, doing their best to move as quietly as possible. The town homes sat in silence, dark and slumbering except for the light on in their kitchen. Elkhorn Cove slept as the night sky lightened with the approaching dawn. Moving as stealthily as possible, Grant and Sam sped through the clearing, into their backyard, and ran into their home, safe from prying eyes and drunks with itchy trigger fingers.

CHAPTER FOUR

Choke (v): Rigging term — A sling made by threading one end of a sling through the eye at the opposite end. A choke may also be made by making a *lark's head* loop with an endless sling.

Choke (v): to deprive a person of air through physical means — to use asphyxiation as a means of sexual arousal.

Grant slept so deeply he didn't remember dreaming. He was awakened at noon by his cellphone ringing. Charlotte was a welcome interruption to his slumber.

"Hey, sleepyhead. You sound like you're still in bed," Charlotte said when he grumbled into the phone. "Are you hungry? How about lunch? Let's go out. I have cabin fever."

"Want to come over here instead? I'll make us lunch. My treat. Eggs, bacon, sausage, hash browns, cranberry juice, and enough coffee to kick start a horse."

"Sold. May I bring along Lina?"

"I didn't expect you to do otherwise. It'll be just the four of us, you, me, Sam, and Lina."

"I can get into that. I haven't been to your house in a long time. I have a surprise for you, too. It's perfect for breakfast."

"Bring it on over. I love surprises."

By the time the clock chimed twelve-thirty, Grant had showered and dressed in his favorite loose black shorts and black t-shirt. Since he worked stage crew, most of his clothing was black. His shorts were so ratty they were falling apart. He had sewn up the seams several times, but he refused to throw them out. They had sentimental value. Sam had bought them for Grant on their first trip to the beach together when they began working crew several years ago. The t-shirt was stretched out of shape. He didn't care. Those clothes were comfortable, like an old shoe, and feeling as out of sorts as he did, he welcomed comfort.

Sam puttered about in the kitchen, eyes at half-mast making coffee. Cobwebs of sleep rested on his face. He seemed to sleepwalk as he poured boiling water into a French press. He had on comfortable clothes he liked to call his rags. Grey loose sweatpants hung from his narrow hips. The loose sleeveless long t-shirt couldn't hide the mass of blond hair growing like a thatch on his chest. Grant loved Sam's half-asleep look.

"Charlotte and Lina are dropping by. You get the coffee cups, and I'll start breakfast," Grant said. He stood behind Sam and slipped an arm around his waist.

"How are you feeling?" Sam asked.

"Groggy, like I'm hung-over. but I didn't drink enough. That was quite a scare we had last night."

"I doubt the drunks knew they were tracking us, or they would have broken down our door by now. I think we're safe. We have to be more careful." Sam stirred the coffee and yawned.

"Let's stick to home tonight. It's safer." Grant patted Sam on the back. "Try to wake up. Don't stumble over the furniture."

Sam leaned against Grant's shoulder. Grant hugged him and gave him a quick buss on the cheek. Sam was his sweetheart. How had lived so long without this beautiful man in his life? He watched as Sam stumbled away, heading for a stool to sit down. Sam could be graceful, but not when he was half awake. Grant grinned, waiting for Sam to stub his toe on the table leg like he did sometimes and let out an adorable streak of cursing. Grant loved everything about Sam, including his tattered morning clothes, his cursing, and his gorgeous body.

"I'll wake up once I have a cup of coffee." Sam yawned again. "You know how I am before caffeine."

"Yes. You're a zombie."

The doorbell rang, and Grant heard the chattering of feminine voices.

"You'd better get the door," Grant said. "I'll get breakfast started."

The mouth-watering scents of frying bacon and savory sausages filled the kitchen. Charlotte, Lina, and Sam sat on tall stools at the breakfast nook. The women had the same mode of dress in mind as Grant. Charlotte pulled her long chestnut hair back in a ponytail. She wore an oversized t-shirt and denim cutoffs. Lina wore her hair loose about her shoulders. She wore a tight tank top that didn't contain enough cloth to cover her huge breasts. Her little purple and white striped shorts weren't much bigger. Charlotte yawned and scratched her head. Watching Charlotte, Lina yawned and stretched.

"Don't do that," Grant said as he tried unsuccessfully to stifle his own yawn. Everyone laughed.

Did they have any idea how sexy they looked? They acted as if nothing was unusual. Charlotte and Lina exuded sex even when they didn't mean to. He watched as Lina opened her mouth in a wide yawn and stretched her torso from side to side. The languid movement made her look like a delectable panther he'd love to ride. She raised her arms in the air to stretch them and caught his eye. She smiled at him, and he blushed in embarrassment having been discovered ogling her. He couldn't help it. She was too beautiful to ignore, and being so nonchalant about it made her even more desirable.

Take her stretching and have Charlotte do it, and there would be a nuclear explosion of lust in his kitchen. Both women looked delicious, and Grant wanted a side dish of Charlotte and a dessert of Lina to go with his breakfast.

Sam had poured coffee, and he drank it faster than anyone else. He walked into the kitchen and poured himself another cup.

"I'm not even halfway finished my first, and you're on your second cup already," Charlotte said.

"He'll drink six cups by the time he's finished," Grant said. "I can't drink that much. My limit is three."

"If I drank six cups of coffee, I'd hum," Lina said.

"If you're quiet and listen hard enough, you can hear Sam hum after he's finished his sixth cup."

"I do not hum," Sam said. "I buzz."

"I start shaking after four cups," Charlotte said. "Too much coffee gives me the jitters."

"If I don't drink it, I *get* the jitters," Sam said.

Charlotte placed a paper bag on the table. "I said I had a surprise for you, Grant. It's actually for both of you, and it's perfect for breakfast."

Grant opened the bag. The scent of pork and savory spices rose from the bag. "Is that what I think it is?" he asked, his mouth watering.

Charlotte smiled. "What do you think it is?"

"It's my favorite. Blood sausage."

"Really?" Sam leaned forward, and Grant swore he would have drooled all over the table if decorum didn't stop him. "We love blood sausage. Where'd you find it?"

"That new meat and cheese shop downtown. Grant, I remember you mentioning that you two liked blood sausage. I picked it up yesterday."

"Thanks. You're too kind."

The dark meat was just what he wanted on a lazy morning,

and there was enough of them to serve all four hungry people. Grant took the two sausages and placed them in a pan with water. They soon sizzled, sending their rich aroma throughout the kitchen.

They made small talk until breakfast was ready. Surrounded by delicious food and intoxicating smells, they dined at the breakfast nook.

"Now this is a traditional English breakfast," Charlotte said. "The only thing missing is the beans."

"I have beans, if you want me to heat them up," Grant said.

"Oh, no, this is fine. More than enough food," Charlotte said. "Thanks for having us over. I've always loved your cooking. It's such a surprise to see a man who cooks this well. You got any other secrets?"

Grant smiled. "There's a lot you don't know about me."

Sam winked at Charlotte. "Me, too."

The women had no idea how accurate those statements were. Grant and Sam kept their shapeshifting a secret to stay out of harm's way, but Grant was growing tired of hiding his wolfen ways. Charlotte and Lina could be special friends if he put his mind to it. He badly wanted to trust someone other than Sam to disclose his secret, but he knew doing so would be far too much of a risk. What if he terrified Charlotte by shifting in front of her, which was the likely outcome? What if the two women turned on him?

Even worse, what if he scared them so much they reported him and Sam to hunters eager to place their heads as trophies on their walls?

He didn't know them well, but he wanted to know them better, which was totally unlike him. Most of the time, he kept to himself with only Sam to keep him company. He loved Sam, but he was lonely. He wanted friends. True friends. Friends to whom he could tell his deepest, darkest secrets, and shifting into werewolf form every month was as deep a secret as he could muster.

How could he start a conversation? He wasn't the most so-cial man on earth. Introverted and shy, Grant stumbled over his words as he tried to make small talk. "So . . ." he said, thinking desperately of something to say that wouldn't sound too stupid. "You two move around a lot?"

"Yes," Charlotte said. "Nothing is permanent."

"We're nomads, and we've been all over the place. We were in Seattle only six months ago. Before that we were in Branson, Missouri working on a musical." Lina sipped her coffee. "Charlotte and I have been thinking of relocating. We're tired of cold winters and everyone calling us hon.

"We've been out east for several years," Charlotte said.

Lina put her arm around Charlotte's shoulders. "Now we're thinking of moving out west. That's one reason we took this gig. We're checking out the Pacific Northwest."

"That's one advantage to our kind of work," Sam said. "We can travel. Try out new locales."

Charlotte smiled. "You're dead-on right. I have wander-lust, although I want to set roots now. Somewhere. I just don't know where yet."

Grant felt hopeful. He liked Portland very much. Why not set down roots? If he could talk Charlotte and Lina into set-tling down, they'd make a mighty foursome. That left Sam.

Charlotte bit into her blood sausage. "Wow, this stuff is good. I've never had it before. It's very minerally."

"Yes, it is," Grant said. "It has that coppery tang to it. Lots of people don't like it." He didn't tell Charlotte he ate it raw. He'd only cooked it this time since eating raw blood sausage in front of the two women would have invited too many ques-tions. "I can thank Sam for discovering it in Chicago a few years back."

"We do love our fancy foods," Sam said. "This is the first time we've run into anyone else who liked blood sausage, though. Every time we've served it for other guests, they gagged."

Grant leaned back and nibbled his hash browns while he watched Sam and the women chatter. Casual conversation shared over breakfast was very pleasant. He could get used to it. Although Charlotte and Lina were two very sensuous women who turned him on sexually, he also enjoyed their company. Both women could take a ribald rude joke, and they even cracked a few of their own. Especially Charlotte, since she was an inveterate tease. Charlotte and Lina also enjoyed the same dark comedies and thriller movies Sam and Grant enjoyed. He and the women worked in the same field. They had similar taste in food. They shared a love for venison, quail, and other game. He wasn't surprised they liked blood sausage. Now to find out what else they had in common.

He stood and walked to his computer. "Want some music?"

"Sure," Lina said. "What kind?"

"I like to listen to something quiet first thing during the day. You two like ambient or trance?"

"New Age." Charlotte clapped her hands. "I love that kind of music. It's so peaceful. You're right. It's perfect for this time of day."

"How about internet radio?" Sam asked. "That way we can put it on and forget about it for the rest of the afternoon."

"Sounds good to me," Charlotte said.

"Me, too," Lina said after sipping her coffee.

The gentle strains of ocean waves set to piano filled the air. Sam made more coffee while Grant and the women cleaned up. Once the dishes were in the dishwasher and coffee brewed, they retired to the living room.

Grant's mellow mood was short-lived, though, once Lina spoke. His fears resurfaced with a vengeance.

"Did you hear about the wolf sighting last night?"

Sam went so pale Grant feared the women would notice, but they didn't.

"What wolf sighting"? Sam asked. Grant hoped the women wouldn't notice the trepidation in his voice.

"Some yahoos saw wolves near the quarry. Four of them."

Four? They must have been seeing double because they were drunk. "What happened to the wolves?" Grant asked, his heart racing.

"They disappeared. The locals are all riled up," Lina said.

"Are they going to start a search party?" Sam asked.

Grant feared the worst.

"Yes. Right now, while it's still daylight. They said it was too hard to see last night even though there was a full moon."

Thank God for that. They didn't get a good look at us or know enough to follow us home.

"I bet they were drunk, too," Grant said. "Couldn't aim for shit. They're more likely to nail a beer than nail a wolf."

Charlotte laughed. "True. They were a bit smashed."

"And you know this . . .how?" Sam asked.

"We went to the Black Horse Pub last night, and they were talking up a storm. Four wolves, according to one. A whole pack according to another. Big as monster trucks. With bright red eyes and sharp, pointy teeth. These wolves sound horrible. Lina and I like to hike along the footpaths. I think we'll steer clear until this business is resolved."

That's a good idea, since *it's risky when we're out and about during the full moon. I don't want to hurt my only real friends. One more night of the full moon, then it's back to normal for another 28 days.*

"Luke was with us. He thinks the guys were drunk and seeing things."

If only that were completely true. "So, he's brushing them off?" Grant asked.

"Not completely," Lina said. "He's sure they saw something. Probably just a couple of large dogs that should have been on leashes. He doubts they saw wolves."

Grant sipped his coffee. "Even if they saw wolves, it's unlikely they'd attack anyone. I understand wolves are shy
around humans, but yeah, it's best to stay off the footpaths at
night until they're either caught or find another place to
hunt." He didn't want to say killed. The likelihood that he
could be felled by bullets terrified him.

"It scares me," Lina said. "I don't like dogs to begin with.
I'm a cat person. That we could run into wolves is too fright-
ening for me to think about."

"I really don't think they'd hurt you," Grant said, trying to
reassure her without saying too much. He felt terrible, knowing he was responsible for her fears. He didn't like scaring his
friends, and he would do anything to rectify the situation.
"Wolves are shy, and they don't attack unless cornered."

Charlotte smiled. "What are you, the wolf whisperer?"

Grant laughed. "I just know my big dogs."

He and Sam would have to be even more careful for the
next twenty-four hours. They'd head for the quarry after
work. That way, they could enter the forest human and shift
once they hit the water. They were much less likely to be seen
in wolf form if they did that.

"Luke told us all kinds of tales last night. Pets have gone
missing over the past few days. brutalized livestock, and hikers are finding partially eaten rabbit and 'possum carcasses
on their trails."

"That can't be right because—" Grant stopped before he
finished his sentence, realizing he'd almost outed himself. He
and Sam had never gone into anyone's backyard, nor had
they harmed any pets. They purposefully avoided pets because they didn't want to call attention to themselves by having to deal with grieving dog and cat owners. They stayed as
deeply in the forest as they could get. Once they'd come close
enough to a neighborhood to see lights in the distance, but

they devoured their kill away from homes and hiking paths.

Something else must have killed those animals.

"Why can't it be right?" Charlotte asked with a confused look on her face.

"Uhm . . .it's because wolves avoid civilization," Grant said. "They wouldn't get so close to a house as to leave kill in a backyard."

"Something's doing it, though," Lina said, her head cocked to one side, eyebrows furrowed.

Grant had better zip his lip before she became suspicious instead of confused.

"You're right." Sam jumped in to help Grant save face. "I think it's a good idea to stay off the hiking paths until the wolf business is cleared up."

"We will," Lina said. "The last thing we want to do is run into a mouthful of sharp teeth surrounded by fur."

Grant was eager to change the subject. "Who wants more coffee? I sure do."

CHAPTER FIVE

R ising Action (n): How the story builds to its climax.
Rising Action (n): Sexual tension between two or more persons.

Sam was sitting on the stage matching gels to frames for the lights when Luke walked in, causing his heart to skip a few beats. The moment Luke twirled he knew Grant could never move with such grace, although Grant wasn't lacking in the grace department. The loose grey sweatpants and black tank Luke wore couldn't hide his powerful physique. He twirled thrice more and ended with a dazzling arabesque so perfect it took Sam's breath away. Luke looked as if he walked on air. He made a series of difficult pirouettes seem so easy.

At the peak of a leap that seemed to make the dancer soar higher in the air than humanly possible, Luke looked down at Sam and gave him a warm smile.

Sam's heart melted into his steel-toed boots.

To his joy and shock, Luke walked to him. "What are you doing?"

"I'm getting your lighting ready for tonight. See the blue and amber gels?" He held up two square gel frames. "The color combination makes you look good."

"All I know is that I stand where I feel the warmth on my face, otherwise I get lost in the shadows." Luke pointed to several circular pieces of metal with cutouts on them called gobos. Some called them cookies because they were the same size and shape as a round cookie. Gobos were placed next to the gel frames to cast patterns of light on the stage. "What patterns are we using tonight?"

"I'm not sure. The lighting director is experimenting with a few shapes. Most likely something swirled to match your movements and your costume."

"I love watching the lights as they take. They make the act something special." He smiled, and if there were anything left of Sam's heart, it would dissolve. "Feel free to watch if you like. I'm going to be doing my most difficult moves tonight."

I'd like to make some moves on you if only you'd let me. "I'll make sure I watch. I'll see if the lighting director will let me light you tonight. That way I can watch you for hours." *Oh, my God, did I just say that?*

Had Luke blushed? He averted his gaze and smiled. "How's Grant? I don't see him here."

"He's out back unloading lamps. Did you want me to get him for you?"

"No, that's okay. I'll catch him later." Voices called from the house. "Ah, that's my cue." Luke said. "It's time to rehearse. Talk to you tonight?"

"You bet you will." Sam winced, hoping he didn't sound too eager. Before he could react, Luke had turned tail and swept away, his tight leotard-clad ass teasing Sam as it moved toward the front of the stage.

"I'm a goner. I have it really bad now. Good thing Grant is open-minded. I am indebted to him for that."

As Sam pulled shutters on the lamps, he watched Luke circulate amongst the other dancers. Hoping he didn't appear to be too stalkerific, he eyed up Luke's muscular legs and taut derriere. His muscles rippled with each step, and once again, Sam was blown over by how such strength belied his grace. Another stubborn lamp refused to cooperate with his focusing. He gave it a swift yank to tame it into position. When he looked back at the stage, Luke was missing. Curious as to where he could have gone, Sam scanned the stage and house but didn't see the dancer.

"If you keep staring at me like that, I'm going to have to take you right here behind the flats."

Gone was the shy dancer who had accosted him only an hour earlier. The man commanded obedience. Sweat beaded on his face, arms, and chest, emitting an animalistic smell that made goosebumps ripple on Sam's arms. While he bore a striking resemblance to Grant, elegant heat and grace poured from every inch of his luscious body in ways Grant could only dream about.

Luke grabbed Sam by the front of his black t-shirt, yanked him against that firm chest, and crushed his lips against Sam's mouth. Gasping for air, Sam succumbed to Luke's fevered embrace. The full moon peeking from behind clouds outside the window pulled at his feral core, and his muscles reacted to his arousal. They pulsed and lengthened, panicking

He who didn't want to shift in the middle of the hottest kiss he'd had in months, not that Grant's kisses weren't hot. They were, but Luke was a shiny new lover, full of bright light and tingling sensations that danced across his lips like static electricity after walking across a plush carpet. His heart leaped as their tongues danced a duet.

His chest cramped as his shift increased, threatening to tear his shirt. Sam breathed deeply, trying in vain to calm his heated arousal. Sensitive to touch, his skin rippled at Luke's feather-like finger brushings. Cool air chilled Sam's arms and hardened his nipples as his skin trembled in savage delight. Luke's arms wrapped around Sam's waist, holding him as he swooned in Luke's embrace.

Sam pressed his groin against Luke's body. An erection strained against Luke's leotard, pressing into Sam's thigh.

Sam lifted his leg to rub his thigh against it, and it jumped. Sam's breath hitched with excitement.

When Luke pulled away Sam whimpered, eager to continue their kiss, but instead of ending their embrace, Luke's lips pressed against his cheek. He ran those soft lips along Sam's jaw until they pressed against the pulse pounding in his throat.

Luke fumbled with the zipper on Sam's black jeans, lowered it quickly, and thrust his hand in. When his fist closed around Sam's hard cock, Sam's body tightened in his arousal. The hair on his head thickened and fell in his eyes. Sam shook his head, fending off the shifting once again. Fear filled his heart that he might turn while in Luke's embrace, scaring him to death, but he refused to pull away from those arousing strokes.

Luke pulled Sam's jeans down to his knees. He squeezed the head at the top of his erection, then fisted tightly at the base. Mouth firmly attached to Sam's throat, Luke held Sam in place with lips and an arm as Sam's vision spun with ecstasy. Lights flashed in Sam's eyes, in time with his pounding heart. He heard a laugh here, a snicker there as people flitted past them, catching a glimpse of Sam caught in Luke's erotic embrace.

Luke grabbed Sam by the arm and pulled him into a narrow space created by two flats hooked together at a cock-eyed angle. Luke went to work between Sam's legs, stroking so quickly Sam feared he'd come all over his jeans. Luke's free hand traveled from Sam's chest to his hips as he lowered himself to face his groin.

When Luke took Sam's cock in his mouth, Sam balled his hands into fists to keep from coming. Luke's tongue flicked around his cock, side to side, making him so hard his breath caught in his throat. When Luke slipped one finger into Sam's asshole, he could no longer contain his bliss, and he shot his load into Luke's mouth, spurting and slamming his hips against his face. Canine teeth lengthened as his pulse pounded in his head, and he let out a deep-throated growl he cut off before it echoed against the walls.

Sam gripped Luke's head with both hands, fucking his sweet mouth until his orgasm subsided. Moving from fevered thrusts to gentle strokes, he slid in and out of that warmth until he grew soft. Breathing deeply, he calmed himself. His teeth receded, and his coarse hair softened until it rested on his head.

Luke rose, wiping the back of his hand against his mouth. Sam blinked his eyes, willing away the glowing yellow that would surely terrify Luke. The muscles in his shoulders shivered as they receded into his resting, human state. His racing heart slowed as afterglow washed over him. Mellow and suddenly sleepy, he winked at Luke. The smile on Luke's rugged face brought forth a grin of relief from Sam.

He has no idea how close he came to seeing me in my wolf form.

"Now that we've been properly introduced, I'm looking forward to midnight even more," Luke said. "I'd love to get to know you and Grant better. Let's take advantage while we can."

CHAPTER SIX

Transformation (n): Becoming the character the actor is portraying.
Transformation (n): The act of shifting between human to wolf form.

Sam and Grant stood in their living room, restless and eager for an hour in the wilderness.

"I need a run. Gotta unwind," Sam said as he stretched his spine. "My back is killing me."

"A run will do both of us some good," Grant said. "Is it wise to head for the woods, though? What about hunters?"

"There's a stretch of woods near the cave where hunting is forbidden. We can run there. I need to get the kinks out of my system." Sam wanted to run to get his blood racing in anticipation of their midnight tryst with Luke. He wanted to taste Luke's sweat after an especially grueling workout. Even after he cleaned up, Sam could sense the masculine pheromones that coursed through such a passionate man after that man had showered. There was nothing as exhilarating as the musk emanating from a man in the heat of passion, whether it was from art or from lust.

"I could use a meal, too. Venison sound good to you?" Sam had worked up quite an appetite all day, and he needed meat. Hunting season promised the most delectable deer meat as long as he and Grant avoided the hunter's arrows. He salivated so much over the thought of a delicious meal of venison, fresh and pink, that he could taste the coppery tang of the blood against his tongue.

Sam stripped off his pants and tossed them against a chair, followed by his shirt and boxer briefs. Naked, he stood in beams of moonlight cast through the living room window that illuminated his wiry arms and well-shaped legs.

He caught the approving expression on Grant's open face. With a smile, he opened his arms to accept Grant as he walked over and slipped his arms around his lover's waist. "We could always forgo the run. Have our own run right here on the rug." He pressed his lips against Sam's and slipped his tongue into his mouth.

Sam closed his eyes, succumbing to the rush of arousal he felt as Grant's kiss overwhelmed him.

That's two hot kisses in one day. Am I a lucky guy or what? "Tempting, lover, but I am in dire need of some fresh air. The run will do us a world of good. Besides, we have a guest at midnight. Witching hour. Plenty of time for a second run on the rug."

Both of them naked, they slid into the night, blending into the shadows as they headed for the woods near the cave where they'd be safe from hunters. Chilled fall air blew against Sam's skin, bringing forth a ripple of shivers until his muscles warmed from exertion. The full moon broke free from the shackles of rain clouds breaking up in the high winds. Stars winked overhead, teasing Sam as they played peek-a-boo with the night haze.

Blood rushed through his veins with the fire of transformation. His breath grew hoarse as his throat tightened and expanded. Limbs lengthened and his back arched, and as he ran, his body pitched forward, forcing him to run on all fours. Legs and arms turned wolfen in their gait and intensity. The rush of adrenaline heated his veins. Thighs and forearms sparked with energy as he raced past low-lying brush and thorny branches so quickly, they stung at his thickening flesh.

Sam never felt as alive as when he sped through the woods in his feral form, and that evening he felt more vibrant than ever.

Hunger raged through him. Deer, warm and bloody, would quench his hunger until midnight, when he would quench his other intense appetite.

Sam, with Grant on his heels, skulked in the underbrush, nose sniffing in search of the gamey scent of buck. His teeth gnashed, mouth drooling with hunger and anticipation. Sam crouched beneath a blackberry bush as a doe and fawn pranced by. *Too small. I need something more substantial.* Sam glanced at Grant, who pawed the earth with sharp claws, as eager for a meal as he was.

As the moon shoved clouds aside to shine full and bright in the night sky, the most majestic buck Sam had ever seen emerged in a clearing. This animal stood nearly ten feet tall with a fifteen-point rack that would make any hunter's heart ache with excitement. The buck's musky scent filled his nostrils, and he resisted snorting lest he scare it into leaping into the woods. This animal would make a magnificent meal. Muscles coiled tense with the hunt as he crawled slowly across the woodland floor until he was within ten feet of the animal.

He bolted. Grant raced immediately behind him, shadowing his moves.

The buck turned tail and scampered through the woods, but it was no match for two werewolves. Within seconds, Sam was on the whimpering beast, biting down on its throat with his massive jaws. He didn't tear flesh with his teeth. Instead, he clamped down with the intention of smothering the animal to death. The buck turned its head towards Sam and stared into his eyes.

Brilliant green eyes, not brown, begged for its life, and there was something familiar about those eyes. He released his grip but held the buck down with his powerful paws.

When he saw the tat on its shoulder, he backed off.

"Grant, stop," he snarled, his body reverting to human form with the shock of recognition. Trees spun around him as his body shrank. He couldn't take his eyes off the buck that stared at him with those amazing emerald eyes, eyes that matched Luke's.

Sam stroked Luke's face as gangly limbs shortened and thickened. His body shrank from its buck form into the familiar human. Eyes wet and wild, breath snorting from flared nostrils, chest heaving in fear and disbelief, a naked Luke lay beneath him, staring at him in all his vulnerability.

"Seems all of us have some secrets," Sam whispered.

Luke nodded, unable to speak.

Grant leaned over Luke as he brushed one hand against fresh cuts on his shoulder. "Are you okay? I'm sorry. We had no idea."

"It's not like I advertise. You couldn't have known." Luke cleared his throat. "I'm fine. Throat's a little hoarse, but that'll pass." He sat up and placed a hand to his forehead. Face pale, he swallowed hard.

He's in shock. We gave him the scare of his life.

Sam felt terribly guilty, and before he could think about what he was doing, he wrapped his arms around Luke ever so gently so not to hurt him or frighten him further. "I'm very sorry. Can you forgive us?"

The smile that crossed Luke's face creased the corners of his shining emerald eyes, revealing sweetness beneath the fear. "For nearly turning me into a meal? It's actually rather comical." His fingers squeezed Sam's wrist with a promise of more to come. He lay in the grass, leaves and twigs entwined in his tousled hair, looking like a god who'd lost his way in the woods. Sam resisted parting his legs and stroking him right there in the grass.

Grant held out his hand, and Luke grasped it. Sam moved out of the way as Grant hoisted Luke to his feet. The two men stood next to each other, looking like the mirror images they were. The moonlight reflected from their glistening skin, cast as marble in the glow of night.

Sam heard whoops and hollers in the distance. They had to get out of the area, fast. "Enough time for pleasure later, lovers. Let's head for the cave. Luke, follow us."

They shifted and raced through the woods, hunters on their tail and the moon showing them the way to safety.

Grant, Sam, and Luke relaxed in human form in the safety of one of the caves behind the quarry. The excitement of the evening stirred adrenaline surged through Sam's veins. Try as he might, he couldn't relax.

"I thought you weren't finished until midnight," Sam said.

"I thought so, too, but the director let me go early. She needed to work with the chorus." Luke brushed his hand against Sam's cheek and squeezed Grant's forearm. "I have more time for both of you now."

"If it weren't for your eyes, I wouldn't have recognized you," Sam said. "Those flashing eyes stand out."

"I know. They're my most fetching feature." Luke stretched out and laid his head in Sam's lap. Grant sat next to Sam with his head resting on his lover's shoulder. He absentmindedly ran his fingers through Luke's tousled hair.

"Were you two behind the wolf sighting last night?" Luke asked.

"Yup. Guilty as charged," Grant said. "Good thing they were totally shit-faced, or they could have easily shot us."

"They were very drunk. I was at the Black Horse Pub last night," Luke said. "They talked of inhuman animals running in the underbrush. No one believed them. The locals do believe there are wolves about, though, so be careful."

"We're trying. I knew you were at the Black Horse. Charlotte and Lina told us," Sam said. "What else did everyone say?"

"They're setting traps. Trying to lure you out with raw meat," Luke said. "They've set out bear traps, too."

"That's not good," Sam said. "Any idea where the traps are? The last thing we need is to get a leg caught in one of those."

"There are three by the Mountain Street hiking paths and two on the other side of the quarry. They placed the traps where they think they saw you last night," Luke said.

"Thanks. That's good to know," Grant said. "Did they bait the traps?"

"Yes. With raw beef."

Sam snickered. "They'd have had better luck with venison."

"I never would have guessed." Luke laughed.

"At least we can sniff out the traps now," Grant said. "It's much easier to do that if they bait the traps."

"Are you two going to be okay?"

"Yes. The full moon doesn't last much longer," Sam said. "We'll get by. We always do." He stroked Luke's forehead and ran his fingers through his hair. Luke's eyes shimmered in the darkness. "You have the most amazing eyes. I've seen green before, but yours are neon."

"I know. Thanks. They came from my mother's side of the family."

"If only my eyes looked like that," Grant said. "Mine are a boring blue."

"Tropical ocean blue, though." Luke said as he stared into Grant's face. "They're quite fetching."

"They're also one of the only ways to tell you two apart," Sam said.

Grant smiled and ran one finger along Luke's cheek. "Did your mother have any kids she didn't tell you about?"

"No, not that I know of." Luke laughed as he stroked

Grant's bare thigh. "I have two younger sisters. They're also dancers."

"Do they shift?" Sam asked.

"Yes, into deer form like me, but smaller. They're does, of course."

All was silent for a moment. When Grant spoke, his voice was quiet. "Do you shift when you make love?"

"No. I've heard of that sort of thing, though. Do you shift?" Luke's eyes were bright with longing.

'Would you like to find out? Grant asked.

The three needed no further encouragement. Strong arms and muscled legs entwined, wrapped around bodies chilled to the touch. Sam's lips found Grant's, parting as tongues met to flirt with each other. Luke's head bobbed up and down as he worked his mouth against Grant's cock, taking it in slowly with such tenderness Sam felt as if Luke's lips had wrapped around his own shaft. Fingers pinched his nipple as his lips pressed against Grant's, tongue seeking out his very soul. Sam's hand alighted on Grant's chest. His heart pounded against his palm, begging to be set free from its cage.

His lover groaned in his mouth as his doppelgänger worked magic on his cock. Sam felt long, slender fingers fondle his balls. Luke's hands, smoother than Grant's calloused ones, rolled his balls, stroked his shaft, squeezed his head. He played until an erect grew in his palm. Sam's chest heaved as he breathed deep, growing in size as his animal instincts took over. His skin tingled whilst his tongue slid over Grant's inner cheeks and Luke stroked him, making his heart skip a few beats.

Muscles in Sam's legs lengthened and tightened while Luke worked on his cock, and Grant gave him the kiss of a lifetime.

Try as he might, Sam's limbs developed minds of their own as feet and hands spread, nails thickened and grew into claws.

He ran his fingers down Grant's back and his claws broke through skin. The coppery scent of blood assailed his nostrils, making his head spin with lust.

The pulse in his neck beat in time with water that dripped from the cave's walls. Luke worked his magic on Sam's cock, switching from hands to mouth. He sucked gently at the head and with tight passion at the base. He cradled Sam's balls, rolling them back and forth over each other. With a guttural cry, Sam came in Luke's hand.

He closed his eyes. The scent of moss and lime floated around his head. Hearing acute as he resisted shifting, he listened. Wind high in the trees searched for sleeping birds. A wildcat yowled in the distance. Skin rough and thick, he shook his body to ward off his changing form. Jagged granite cut into his back, rigid and unforgiving, and he dragged his back against the sharp corners, pain bringing him back to his human senses.

Sam relaxed as his body settled back into its human form. His senses acute to every sound and flash of light, he breathed slowly and deeply until he calmed down. Rain pattered fallen leaves on the soft ground. Lightning streaked across the sky, flooding the woods with a wash of brightness.

"We should get going before the rain lets up," Grant said over the din. "We can get past hunters easier in a shower."

Rain washed away animal scents, as did the quarry water, making it harder for hunting dogs and the local rednecks to track the three shifters. As Sam followed Grant around trees and shrubbery to their home, with Luke on his heels, the woods closed in, darkness enveloped him, and isolation pillowed over them like a flimsy blanket on a cold bed.

All I ever do is run. I'm tired of running. I want to walk outside without having to look over my shoulder. Why can't I watch the skies at night without worrying about when the next full moon will be? Why can't I rest?

The loneliness of isolation wrapped around him like a

straitjacket, restricting his breathing until he choked with sadness. Sam didn't have the heart to tell Grant how he felt. What would it take for him and Grant to settle down?

Could Luke, Charlotte, and Lina help them make roots?

Grant sifted through CDs. "Anything in particular you'd like to hear? I have techno, trance, hard rock, acid rock, ambient, New Age . . ."

Luke took a pull from his beer. "Some sexy techno music. So perfect to set the right mood, don't you think?"

Racing techno beat the air, setting of sparks of excitement in Sam. He patted the couch cushion next to him, smiling at Luke. Crimson burned Luke's cheeks as his mouth spread into a smile, creasing his delightful dimples.

His shyness makes me tingle all over. How endearing.

Luke's emerald eyes flashed when Sam stole a glance at him as he sat next to him. "Help yourself to the junk food." Sam pointed to the coffee table.

"Oh, boy, munchies." Luke grabbed the bag and popped a chip in his mouth.

"We call them Styrochips. They're like crack," Sam said.

"You have cheese sticks, too. I rarely see those," Luke said.

Grant tossed a bag to Luke, who caught it in mid-air. "Help yourself. We buy only the best crap."

"How long have you two been together?" Luke asked.

Was Sam imagining it, or did Luke seem out of breath? Luke's arm brushed against Sam's, and the heat emanated from his body, scorching Sam's skin. Sam licked his lips, his mouth suddenly dry.

Lust does that to a person. Makes you thirsty for something sweet and warm.

"We've been together for several decades. For the past ten years, we've opened our relationship. We like having a third person to play with."

"Has that person always run on all fours through the

forest?"

Caught off guard, Sam coughed up an uncomfortable laugh. "No, not normally. You took us by surprise."

"I was born a shifter. My mother is fae, and my father is human. How about you two?"

"We were changed," Grant said. He drank his beer. "I met my fate in Germany."

"Grant changed me," Sam said.

Luke's eyebrows shot up in surprise. "Really? I suppose that didn't go over well at first."

"Actually, it did. We fell in love, and I asked him to change me. I wanted to be with him forever, and now we are." Sam flashed back to the night he asked Grant to change him. "I was a lighting tech at a strip club in Vegas when I met Grant. I fell hard and fast."

"Our first full moon together, I shifted in front of him by accident and nearly scared him to death."

"Two months later, I asked him to change me. Here I am today, just as gorgeous and as young as ever." Sam laughed.

"You *are* gorgeous. I suspect you're much older than you look," Luke said. "How old are you, if you don't mind my asking?"

"I was born in 1896, changed in 1931." Grant said. "I was thirty-five when I changed."

"Grant changed me in 1970. I was born in 1942. I was twenty-eight and in love." He wrapped his arms around Grant's strong body and nestled into his shoulder. "Never looked back."

"You're not exclusive?"

"Nope." Grant grinned. "We started out that way, but it got boring fast. Plus, we swing both ways, so we're always on the lookout for fresh meat."

Luke's throaty laugh rumbled in his throat. "In more ways than one."

"Oh, we avoid humans. We like game."

"I know. You almost ate me."

"We sure dodged a bullet there," Sam said. "Speaking of eating, I'm famished. All this excitement worked up my appetite."

"As long as it's not venison." Luke gave Sam a cheeky grin, so full of mirth Sam snickered.

"When I eat you, you'll love it," Sam said, and his pulse raced as the expected flush washed over Luke's rugged features. "How about steak? It's quick and easy."

"I don't eat meat," Luke said.

"Of course you don't." Grant pulled a jar of tomato sauce out of the pantry. "How about pasta? I have spinach raviolis I made last week in the freezer. More than enough to feed three people."

"Sexy and he can cook. No wonder Sam loves you. I crave ravioli. Thanks for feeding me."

"It's the least we can do after nearly making a meal out of you." Grant tapped his beer bottle. "Refill?"

"Yes, I'd love one."

By the time they sat down to eat, Sam was so hungry he could have eaten the plate the ravioli came on. The three enjoyed a sumptuous meal by candlelight with trippy techno playing in the background.

Ah, this is the life. This is what I want. Grant, and Luke, and a good meal. I can get used to this.

Sated, the three of them returned to the living room. Sam and Luke sat on the couch while Grant sat in a plush chair next to them.

"Dinner was delicious," Luke said. "You're an excellent cook, Grant."

"Thank you. I'm glad you enjoyed it." Grant's voice mellowed in his relaxation.

Sam expected him to fall asleep in the chair like he did so

often on the couch after a big dinner.

"I'm surprised we're not fat." Sam closed his eyes and breathed deeply, enjoying the full feeling of a sumptuous meal. "Then again, as much crew work as we do, we burn off the pounds quickly enough."

"Do you feel sated, Luke?" Grant's deep voice rumbled with a promise of much more.

"Yes, I do."

"So . . . How about we sate your other appetites?" Sam slipped his hand between Luke's legs, squeezing his inner thigh. Without needing an invitation, Luke's lips pressed against Sam's throat, soft pillows caressing his skin. Sam closed his eyes, taking in Luke's animal scent and masculine heat. A tongue moistened his skin, making him jump.

He turned toward Luke, who lifted Sam's t-shirt over his head. Luke attacked him with gusto, tongue flicking against his right nipple until it hardened. Sam's cock strained against his jeans, and his fingers tore at the zipper until Luke squeezed his hands, setting them aside. With one deft motion, he unzipped Sam's jeans and slid a hand inside. When his fingers wrapped around Sam's stiffening cock, Sam fisted Luke's hair and pressed his head downward.

The scent of sweat and musk floated around his head, and he opened his eyes. Luke worked his magic on Sam, bringing Sam's cock to full attention. As Luke sucked, Grant's cock bobbed inches from Sam's face, seeking the warmth of his mouth. Sam slipped Grant's cock past his lips as Luke's tongue flickered back and forth around his own shaft. Once Grant was stiff and purple with arousal, he pulled out, making Sam whimper, wanting to relish Grant's salty flavor.

"Let's head for the shower. We can get clean—and play," Grant said.

In the shower, Sam's body entwined with Grant's and Luke's, his hands seeking supple flesh. The crisp scent of peppermint floated on the steam as he poured bath gel on a mesh pouf. Pressing Luke by the shoulder to turn him around, he ran the pouf over his muscular back, tendons twitching as the rough material moved over his skin. Sam loved the feel of Luke's soft skin against his rough fingers. Such young skin on a man who couldn't have been more than twenty-two to Sam's twenty-eight. Grant's fingers massaged shampoo in his hair, piling it high on his head as the suds flowed down his face. Sweet orange scent sailed up his nose, making his nostrils curl with delight.

Sam felt Luke's hand at his backside. He clenched around the slender finger that slid so easily into his anus. Luke's warmth encircled his cock as Sam leaned against the shower wall, each droplet of hot water stinging his skin as it splashed hard over him. Luke's mouth worked his shaft, sucking with increased intensity as he took in Sam's entire cock. Luke's finger slid in to the bottom knuckle, impaling, probing, and finding Sam's most sensitive spot. He slid in a second finger, and Sam grasped his head by each side, guiding Luke's mouth over his rigid cock. His smooth movements mirrored Grant's style, and Sam looked at the lithe yet muscular man who knelt before him as if honoring a god.

They are so much alike.

Luke sucked with a tenderness that enhanced the passion pouring from his very being. Sam caressed his head, running his fingers through hair as thick as Grant's. Luke released Sam's cock from his mouth, and not without a little groan of disappointment from Sam, but when Luke stared up at Sam with those shining emerald eyes, Sam's heart flipped somersaults in his chest.

Sam gazed at the countenance looking up at him, such an open and naïve trusting face on such a knockout of a body. As he basked in Luke's gaze, Luke stroked his cock, pulling hard. Sam warmed so much over the bald expression of affection on Luke's face that his orgasm overcame him. He spurted against his stomach, overcome by passion washing over his body. Lights flashed before his closed eyelids, and his pulse throbbed in his throat. Waves of orgasm flowed through his limbs with each wave easing until he leaned back against the wall, exhausted from the exertion.

Grant wrapped his arms around Sam, pressed their mouths together, and spread his lips apart with his tongue. Spinach and hops rolled in his mouth, reawakening his senses.

"Are you ready for a movie, lover?" Grant nibbled on his ear, making him jump.

"Our guest should choose."

"Our guest should stay the night."

"I'd like that." Luke's fingernails ran down Sam's back, eliciting shivers of pleasure.

"Let's head for the living room. I have an extra set of clothes for you, Luke," Grant smiled. "We're about the same size."

"Might as well be twins," Luke said.

Sam watched the two men as they dried each other's bodies with clean, thick towels. Muscles throbbed with each movement. Black hair glistened wet in the soft light. Luke turned toward Sam and smiled, emerald eyes flashing promises of more to come. Sam knew he wasn't going to get much sleep.

CHAPTER SEVEN

Head Shot (n): A professional photograph of a person from the shoulders up. Used for resume purposes.
Head Shot (n): Oral sex on a man.

Sam dried off and wrapped a towel around his waist when the doorbell rang.

Who would be calling at two o'clock in the morning?

Curious, he walked to the door and looked through the peephole. Charlotte and Lina filled his line of vision, distended and elongated from the fisheye lens effect of the peephole as if they were reflected in a funhouse mirror. With those two around, life *was* like a rollercoaster ride at a carnival. He opened the door.

Charlotte's eyebrows flipped up, and she gave a low wolf whistle. "Wow, and he comes gift wrapped already for us."

Sam forgot he wore only a towel around his waist.

"May we come in? We come bearing gifts." Lina peered at him from over Charlotte's shoulder, a mischievous grin spreading across her face.

"How'd you know we'd be up? We might have been asleep."

"Fat chance of that, luv." Charlotte pushed her way past Sam.

The crisp scent of seagrass and moss from her shampoo and body lotion drifted in the air around him. Sam admired the swing of her shapely ass as she sauntered through the living room into the kitchen, followed by Lina who floated in a cloud of spring rain and freshly mown grass.

They just showered. How I would have loved to be in that shower with them, soaping up their backs and getting them clean inside and out. Even better, a hot, steamy shower with them, Luke, and Grant would satisfy me no end. If only the shower was the size of a two-car garage.

"We know you two aren't alone, so we invited ourselves over again for another party." Charlotte said.

"What's in the bag?" Grant tried to take the bag from Charlotte's arms, but Lina slapped him away.

"Get off. It's time to play Show-And-Tell." Lina pulled a bottle from the bag. "Cognac! Let's do some serious drinking."

"Are you *trying* to get us shit-faced?" Grant asked.

"I can't get you shit-faced without your permission."

Lina sat the bottle of cognac, a bag of pepper salami, pheasant, pâté vegetarian quiche for Luke, apple butter, five bright red apples, and a wedge of brie on the kitchen table. Charlotte placed a loaf of French bread next to the delightful food. Sam's mouth watered with anticipation of another night of sinful decadence with his lovely co-workers.

Charlotte nibbled on a piece of salami as if she was making love to it.

Lina had been there so often she knew where everything was in the house. She walked to the kitchen, found five snifters, and poured brandy for all of them.

Sam's cock bobbed beneath his towel, eager for Round Two.

"How about we get this party rolling?" Charlotte asked.

Sam left the room long enough to put on a t-shirt and jeans. By the time the five of them made it to the living room, Sam overheated from the sexual possibilities before him.

Wouldn't do to sit around wearing only a bath towel, no matter how comfortable it is.

"Good thing we have off today. We're going to need the rest." Grant sipped his cognac.

"I don't think we'll be getting much rest tonight. I'm feeling adventurous." Charlotte dipped her finger in her cognac and rubbed it around her mouth, pursing her lips with the promise of much more.

"Charlotte, you're such a tease," Luke said. "I don't know how you get away with it."

"I'm utterly charming," she said. "I can't help myself. Here you go." After handing Luke a slab of quiche, she sliced some bread. "Who wants pâté? Anyone want brie and an apple slice?"

Sam realized he was starving. All the earlier exertion gave him an appetite. "I'll take the pâté. I haven't had pheasant in a while."

She spread pâté on a slice and handed it to Sam. Grant helped himself to brie on bread with a sliver of apple on top. Once Lina and Luke filled their plates with hors d'oevres, the five sat down. Charlotte, Lina, and Luke chose the couch, Sam and Grant on chairs.

"Have you heard? There's been another sighting about an hour ago," Lina said. "A bunch of teenagers saw a wolf when they were on bike paths in the woods."

Sam knitted his brows. They couldn't have seen him and Grant, since they'd been home all evening with Luke. What had the kids seen? Assuming they saw anything, since telling everyone within earshot you saw wolves would bring them lots of attention. Knowing kids, that was exactly what they would want, but somehow, Sam knew that wasn't the case.

"This isn't the first sighting, either. It's been seen for the past couple of weeks, but no one has been able to catch it." Charlotte said.

"I thought wolves traveled in packs," Luke said.

"They do," Grant said.

"Has it hurt anyone?" Sam asked, dreading the answer.

"No, but it killed some livestock, which is why the farmers and hunters are after it. Hikers had found 'possum, raccoon, and woodchuck carcasses for weeks, and they didn't bat an eye. Once the sheep started getting mauled, the rifles came out."

Sam felt a pang of distress. What if this was another werewolf? It must have felt terribly frightened and lonely, being trapped in Portland without any support at all. Sam would not have survived if it weren't for Grant never leaving his side, showing him how to care for himself, how to hunt, and how to blend in. The last thing Sam wanted to do was to live this troubling life alone.

Assuming this was a werewolf, it had made a huge mistake in killing and partially eating livestock. Farmers didn't like losing money. Gutting a cow or sheep called attention to oneself. If only he could meet this wolf and help it. It would be good to meet another kindred spirit. How could he discover its identity? He doubted it was a local. The killings had been going on for only a couple of weeks. He suspected they'd started at about the time the troupe had arrived in Portland. How could he draw out the shifter and let it know it had kindred spirits who would help it? At the very least, he could teach it to leave the livestock and pets alone. Killing those animals guaranteed a rifle in the snout in the near future.

"Where exactly has the wolf been seen?" Sam asked.

"Near the Mountain Street hiking paths," Lina said.

That was not good. The location was too out in the open.

"One of the hunters shot it last night," Charlotte said. "Nicked the shoulder, but it kept on running."

Panic surged in Sam's veins. He had to know if this was another werewolf.

"It's scary," Lina said. "I like to hike along those paths, but now I can't. I'm too afraid of running into a beast."

You won't have to worry after tonight, at least for another month.

"Maybe it can be caught and relocated," Sam said. "I hope it isn't killed."

"I'm for moving it to a more secluded location, away from people," Charlotte said.

"Let's stop talking about wolves and shootings. I'm getting depressed," Grant said as he poured himself another glass of cognac.

"Let's talk about sex," Luke said with a grin.

Charlotte laughed. "I'm game."

"Me, too," said Lina.

"Okay, spill it," Luke said, "Charlotte, have you gone through the entire troupe yet?"

"Of course not," she said with mock indignation. "I'm very picky. My partners have to be special and exciting. I've rejected most advances. Hey, I chose *you*, after all."

"All three of us," Sam said.

"We're both very satisfied with our choices." Lina said, then nibbled on a sliver of apple. Her pointed tongue slipped out and grabbed a morsel of apple on her lip. It was a tiny movement, but oh so sexy. "But we're not here for an orgy tonight. At least, I'm not."

"Me, neither. I'm here for the food and good company," Charlotte said.

Sam had to smile at her statement. He'd met acquaintances at most theaters, but the camaraderie ended when the curtain fell for the final time. Those who had been close even to the point of enjoying each other's bodies parted and went their separate ways. It was a bit different for crew members, since they tended to travel together from show to show, and they often worked together on subsequent shows. Tech crew could be very clannish and protective, unlike actors. He'd grown close to various crew members on occasion, but the deep level of comfort he felt with Charlotte and Lina thrilled him. He'd rarely experienced such closeness, and he did not take their friendship for granted.

Sam and Charlotte cleaned up while Luke put on a new CD and Grant used the bathroom. Standing in the kitchen, Charlotte spoke and took Sam completely by surprise.

"Lina's working on the set tomorrow. I have the afternoon off. Would you and Grant like to come over for dinner?"

"We'd love to, but Grant is working tomorrow. Do you mind only one of us?"

"Definitely come over. We can make it a twosome. A date." She grinned. "I'd ask Luke, but he's rehearsing tomorrow. Then again, it would be nice to catch you alone for a change."

Was she flirting with him? It wasn't like they hadn't enjoyed each other's bodies before. This somehow felt different. Charlotte seemed almost shy about asking him over. He wondered what that was all about.

"Then it's a twosome. I'll bring wine. Red or white?" Sam asked.

"Red. I'm serving lamb chops."

"I love lamb chops."

"Good. I broil them to perfection."

"My mouth is watering just thinking about it. It's a date."

She grinned, blushed, and walked into the living room. He'd finally have Charlotte alone. How he'd longed for a chance to play with her without any other partners present. She was quite the daring type, but there was a core to her that was very private. Charlotte was a conundrum — extroverted and vivacious while at the same time secretive and shy. She only let him see what she wanted him to see. Nothing else. Could he get closer to her, get her to expose parts of herself she rarely let see the light of day? What kind of lover was she when she wasn't goofing off or testing her limits and his limits? Charlotte loved her sex toys, shackles, and whips, but Sam suspected she hid behind her gear so she wouldn't expose too much of herself. Granted, he enjoyed the gear, but he wanted to engage Charlotte's soul. That would take a bit of encouragement.

The five friends enjoyed each other's company until five, when they parted ways. Lying in bed, Sam couldn't help but think about the mysterious wolf. It nudged its way into his thoughts, even interrupting his pleasant dreams about Charlotte. It had appeared near Mountain Street? Could he talk Grant into tracking it down? His curiosity would get the better of him. Sam knew he would not rest well until he met this wolf face to face.

CHAPTER EIGHT

Grip (n): Rigging and lighting technicians in film and video production. They also work closely with camera operators.

Grip (v): To grab, to hold

Rainclouds darkened the dusk sky. Sam hiked along the trails where the other wolf had been spotted, hoping he would catch a glimpse of it. He raced past sticker bushes that scratched at his bare forearms with thorns that left faint red marks but did not break the skin. Toadstools clustered at the base of maple and oak trees. He knew better than to eat them. At least these weren't the hallucinatory kind. He'd stumbled upon the trippy ones in the southwest and ever since then he'd avoided eating any mushroom in the wild. As he rushed down the path, he inhaled the crisp autumn air. It smelled of moss and pending rain. His entire body reacted to his surroundings as the breeze brought forth goosebumps. He felt gloriously alive, and he relished his time in the woods. Even when not in wolf form, he enjoyed a leisurely hike. He wondered if the other wolf felt the same way.

"Do you think we'll find it?" Sam asked.

"I hope so. It doesn't know how dangerous things are out here if it hangs out on the biking paths," Grant said.

Sam wondered how long the wolf had been in Portland. He didn't recall any sightings last month. Maybe the wolf had subsisted on smaller woodland animals and avoided livestock. The big mistake it made this month was mauling a few sheep. In calling attention to itself, it set the locals on high alert, which put him and Grant in much more danger than usual. He wanted to partially shift so he could sniff out the wolf with more ease.

That was assuming it was a werewolf. He couldn't know for sure.

"Do you think we drank enough rye to control the shifting?" Grant asked.

"Yes. I'm going to do a partial now. It'll be easier to track the wolf if I can catch a whiff of it."

Sam relaxed his body, which helped him to shift comfortably. As long as he shifted only slightly, his clothing wouldn't tear. It wouldn't do for him to wander into town with a torn shirt and jeans. His arms and legs lengthened, growing more muscular with each inch. As his face molded into that of a wolf, his vision intensified. Sounds became much clearer, and he heard noises he wouldn't have heard in human form. Mingling with the pleasant pine and clean air scent, he smelled the aroma of various animals. One scent stood out — the unmistakable scent of a shifter. Shifter scent depended on the type of creature to which one shifted. In the case of a wolf, the scent reminded him of a cross between sweat and blood.

He hugged the ground on all fours and followed the scent trail beyond the biking trails. Deep in the woods, with Grant on his tail, Sam ran, the night air blowing against the sensitive skin on his face. His hair had lengthened, but he wasn't completely covered.

Listening to the wind blow through the trees, he heard a deeper, crackling sound of a large creature breaking branches and crushing leaves as it made its way through the woods. He followed the sound with Grant on his heels. They soon came upon the side of the quarry that faced more biking paths. Ahead of them, in the brush, Sam saw a dark figure crouching amid a copse of wild blackberry bushes.

He stopped running. Grant stopped and stood not far behind him. Sam stared into the twisted branches until he saw bright yellow eyes blinking at him. He walked toward the bushes, ever so slowly, hoping to not scare the creature away. It didn't move. All it did was sit amid those thorns and berries, staring back at them.

"We're not going to hurt you." Sam called, hoping his voice wasn't so loud it attracted human attention.

It only crouched, staring.

"Hello? You can come out. We won't hurt you."

"Go away." A light, soft voice. This wolf was a female.

"Who are you? We can help you. Let us approach you." Sam said. She shuffled in the brush. "Don't run away. We want to talk to you. We know what you are. We're the same thing."

"Leave me alone. I don't know you." The fear in her voice tore at Sam's heart.

"We work at the theater," Grant said.

"You do? So do I."

Who was she? Sam didn't recognize her voice. He didn't think she was one of the crew.

"Are you a dancer?" Sam asked.

"Yes. I'm in the chorus. I'm new."

He didn't know the dancers well, aside from Luke. Which ones were new? He recalled a handful of women who seemed less experienced and familiar than the others. One with long black hair she wore in a ponytail often gorged on the brownies from craft services. She had one hell of a sweet tooth. He didn't think she was the shifter, because she seemed so at ease with the entire cast. She didn't give off wolf vibes. Another wore her purple hair short in the back and longish in the front. The little gamine also did not give off wolf vibes. She'd proven to be one of the more popular members of the troupe.

Sam had smiled when he saw her flirt earlier that day with yet another dancer. The woman had her pick of any man in the troupe. If she was bi, he was certain Charlotte would make a play for her. She seemed to be Charlotte's type. Sam recalled several other dancers stretching in the wings. Sam had watched a blonde raise her leg over her head. A gorgeous African American woman who wore her hair in many braids slid so comfortably into a split Sam wondered if she had any bones in her legs. Maybe the shifter was one of them.

"You can tell us who you are. We won't hurt you."

"I don't know you. I can't. I'm scared."

"When did you change?"

"I can't tell you. Please, leave me be. I want to be left alone."

"It's not safe here. Too many people use the bike paths," Grant said. "You're taking a great risk running on this side of the quarry."

"I know, but I have nowhere else to go. I can't control myself."

"We can show you safe places to hide until after the full moon," Sam said. "Do you have a mentor?"

"No. I'm alone."

He took a few steps toward her.

"Stay back." She stepped out from behind the bushes on her hind legs. She was on the small side, certainly smaller than he was. Her fur was an enviable auburn, thick and lush. The red wolf crawled along the ground on all fours, then stood upright. Her resigned dignity gave her a hopeless air, as if she wanted to be caught.

"We can help you," Grant said.

"No one can help me." A hollow sound of desolation filled her voice. Her tone tore at Sam's heart. How he yearned to help her. He couldn't unless she let him into her world.

"What's your name? I'm Sam Hightower, and he's Grant Newsome."

"I have no name."

Sam took a step toward her, and she took a step backward.

"I don't want to live like this." Her voice wavered, and Sam saw she was shivering. He couldn't tell whether she shivered from the night chill or from fear.

"None of us do, but it's easier to take if you have some support. When you are with your own kind, you're safer."

"You aren't my kind. I'm human."

"Not now you aren't," Sam said.

"Don't piss her off. She'll bolt." Grant whispered in Sam's ear.

"When were you turned?"

"Two months ago. It wasn't here. I was working in Vegas when I was attacked."

She's new. No wonder she's scared. She needs support, and we can give it to her. If only she weren't so damned stubborn. Sam remembered how stubborn Grant had said he was when he first changed. He'd desperately wanted help, but he was too afraid to seek it. He somehow survived on his own until he found his own mentor, who sadly was killed in a knife fight. Grant had supported Sam from the start, and Sam knew how lucky he was. This wolf needed someone in her corner, if she would allow him in.

"You don't have to go through this alone. We know how scary it is when you're first starting out. Please let us help you."

"I don't want your help." The resignation in her voice stabbed at Sam's heart. He knew what she wanted, but he couldn't face the probability.

She wanted to die.

As if she heard Sam's thoughts, she whirled about and raced through the woods heading toward the biking paths. What on earth was she doing, running right into the hunter's vicinity? What if she stepped on one of those bear traps?

"We have to find her," Sam said.

"If she doesn't want our help, we can't do anything for her."

"I know, but she's scared."

"She won't last long if she stays close to the biking trails."

'I think that's the point." Sam said. "She's lost her will to live."

"We can't follow her. Not where she went, with hunters, drunks, and God knows what else out looking for wolves. All of us will be killed if we take that chance. Let's head home. We're safer there."

They raced through the woods, beyond the quarry and the safety of the caves. Sam couldn't stop thinking about the terrified little wolf. He wanted to help her. If only he knew who she was. As he replayed her voice in his mind, he thought about all the dancers of his acquaintance. None were familiar. He hung out with crew, not dancers. He recalled a couple of very pretty brunettes, but he doubted any of them was his wolf. *His* wolf? Was she really his? No, she wasn't, but he thought of her that way. He wanted to protect her, to be a mentor to her the way Grant had for him all those years ago. Those brunettes seemed very comfortable in their own bodies, and they mingled well with dancers and even crew. Dancers and crew usually lived in their separate worlds. Seldom did they mingle. Luke was a rarity in that respect. Sam suspected his dancer was of a lighter complexion as well. How many redheads were amongst the dancers? He couldn't recall a single one, which didn't surprise him since he wasn't into gingers.

Upon nearing home, they shifted into human form. They walked through their backyard without so much as a dog barking. Once inside, Sam poured them both some brandy, and they sat in the backyard.

"She's not going to make it," Grant said. "We can't help her if she won't accept our help."

"We can't let her go about out there by herself. Do you think Luke may know who she is?"

Grant nodded with a concerned look on his face. He worried about her, too. That was like Grant, to worry about someone in need, especially a fellow shifter, since he and Sam rarely met one. If only they could learn her identity.

"Maybe. He straddles both worlds quite well," Grant said. "He knows most of the dancers, and he hangs out with crew. Do you remember any redheads?"

"No. You know I prefer my lovers tall, dark, and gorgeous." He smiled and rested a hand on Grant's thigh. "She could look like Marilyn Monroe and I wouldn't notice."

"I seriously doubt that."

"Okay, maybe not Marilyn, but I don't do redheads."

"Let's ask Luke about her the next time we see him. I hope he has some answers." Grant took Sam's hand in his and gave it a squeeze. Responding to the intimate touch, Sam curled into Grant's body. Knowing his wolf was in danger made him feel closer to his own lover and mentor.

"If she goes on much longer on her own like this, with drunks brandishing guns running about, she won't last past nightfall," Sam said, concern clouding his relaxing mood.

They drank in silence. Sam worried for her fate, but there was nothing he could do about it this morning. The last night of the full moon was tomorrow. If he could track her down again and talk her into befriending them, she had a better chance. Deep down he knew she hated the shifter side of herself, and she wanted to be rid of it.

By ten that morning, he was in bed, fighting off fitful dreams of a lovely auburn wolf crying in the wilderness, and he couldn't find her.

CHAPTER NINE

Fly (n): (see Fly System) A system of ropes, pulleys, counterweights and similar objects within a theater that enables a stage crew to safely, quickly, and quietly hoist items such as curtains, scenery, lights, stage effects and, occasionally, people.
Fly (n): An opening in trousers that is closed by a zipper or by buttons concealed under a fold of cloth.

Knowing they could trust Luke, Grant called him and asked if he and Sam could come over for a visit and some advice. Luke acquiesced, and within fifteen minutes Sam and Grant sat on a plush couch in front of a roaring fire in Luke's living room. The room was spacious but cozy. Oriental rugs covered the floors. A painting of geese flying over a lake covered the wall opposite the couch above a fireplace. Fire crackled in the hearth. The wooden walls and plaster ceiling with wooden beams gave the chalet a warm and comforting feeling. The rustic chalet brought forth a craving for hot cocoa and marshmallows, which Luke served on a hand-carved oak coffee table.

"Do you know of a dancer, a young woman who may be new, who came over from Vegas?" Grant asked.

"Yes, there are three of them. Melissa, Cheyenne, and Willow. Why do you ask?"

"Because your lone wolf the drunks have seen is one of them." Sam said.

Luke's face broadened in astonishment. "Really? How do you know this?"

"We met her last night near the walking paths," Sam said. "She's not in good shape. We have to track her down and get her to trust us before she gets herself killed."

"That's another problem," Grant said. "We think she wants to die. She's very green. She was turned when she was in Vegas, and she's completely alone."

Grant felt protective of the young wolf, even though he didn't know her. Perhaps because he didn't know her, he felt her vulnerability. Although he wasn't a part of a pack, he felt the intense stirrings of pack instinct in wanting to keep her out of harm's way. If he could help her overcome her fear and dejection, maybe he could come to terms with his doubts and troubled feelings about his own ability to shift. The monkshood rye concoction did more than prevent him from fully shifting. It gave him a feeling of control over his life, although it was false security. The drink only staved off the inevitable. He was a werewolf, and he would shift during the full moon. In fact, he needed to shift. If he didn't, he came down with the most unbearable headaches. Besides, shifting in some ways was incredibly freeing. He could soar through the woods at breakneck speed and take in all the scents and sounds around him with his wolf senses that were much more enhanced than his human senses. Despite his misgivings, he liked shifting.

"I don't know any of them well, so I can't even begin to guess which one is the shifter." Luke said, then a pensive expression crossed his face. "Willow's very shy, though. She seems scared of her own shadow."

"Which one is Willow?" Grant asked.

"She's a tiny little redhead, wispy voiced, and she doesn't play well with others. She sticks to herself. Not much of a partier, although she does go to the Black Horse Pub with the dancers sometimes. I haven't seen her there over the past two nights, though."

Grant didn't recognize the description. He had no idea which dancer she could be. If Willow wanted to make herself invisible, she had accomplished her goal.

"Our wolf is red. She may be Willow," Sam said. "We need to corner her and feel her out, but we have to be careful. If she's not the wolf, we could give ourselves away too quickly."

"I don't know her, either," Grant said. "Sam is visiting Charlotte today, but I'll be tending to the lamps. Are you dancing tonight, Luke?"

"Yes."

"We need to confront her. If we can get her to trust us, we can talk her into being careful."

"That's assuming Willow is the shifter."

"True. Let's keep an eye on all three women and feel them out."

Chapter Ten

Pack (n): A sound/radio device with microphone, batteries, and transmitter pack that's used most often in musicals where the singers must be amplified so that the audience may hear them over the orchestra. In shows that aren't musicals, these devices are used to reinforce speech.

Pack (n): a group of wolves.

Sam drove to Charlotte and Lina's home with a lump in his throat.

How am I going to act once I stand in her living room? She invited me, not the other way around.

He checked his smile in the rearview mirror. The whitening strips had done their job. Eating raw meat and drinking blood had a tendency to stain his teeth.

She's different from other women. Unpredictable and aggressive, she's a go-getter—completely different from the soft and quiet types I normally go for. I was so touched when she fed me her homemade matzo ball soup last week when I was sick. That was totally against character. She isn't the caregiver type, but she fed me. That has to count for something.

I see her as my equal. Hell, in many ways she's better than me. I'm only a lighting technician. What she does takes real talent. She's an artist. She goes after what she wants. I do the same, but I feel so intimidated by her.

By the time Sam pulled into the parking spot behind Charlotte's sports car, he was a quivering bundle of nerves. He checked his watch—five. He had three hours before dark. Plenty of time to hang out until he had to leave.

Why am I so tense? There's nothing to be afraid of. I even brought a bottle of wine and flowers. Is that going overboard? Too much too soon? I hope not. I have a feeling she's the one. I can trust her with my big secret. I've been badly burned before. Justin, for instance. He didn't tell me he was in a closed relationship with a guy I didn't even know existed. I should have known something was up when he wouldn't allow me to visit him at his home. I fell for his joke that his house was one step away from being declared condemned by the Board of Health. I found out the truth when I called him one evening, and Sid answered the phone. I didn't want to mess with Sid after Justin told me about him. The man was a psycho hose-beast who was jealous of anyone Justin so much as sneezed at. Still, Justin never told me about him. I don't cheat. It's annoying, dishonest, and it shows he didn't really care about me. He didn't take me seriously. I was just a plaything to him, and there I was, falling for him. Never again. No married people or those involved in closed relationships, even if they try to convince me their partners are okay with it. The next time I hear that line, I'll ask to speak to the partner. I've avoided much grief by standing my ground. I won't let that happen again. I have a feeling I have nothing to fear with Charlotte, but I have to feel her out first. That'll take some time.

"Oh, how sweet." Charlotte said when she opened the door. "Chianti and zinnias. How'd you know I love zinnias?"

"I didn't. They just looked nicer than the other flowers. There were the usual daisies and carnations dipped in dye colors that don't exist in nature. I thought you'd like the zinnias. These are huge. They look like sea anemones. Consider them a thank you present for inviting me over."

"Let me put them in water. I'll get us some glasses, too. I hope you're famished. I'm just finishing dinner."

Sam smelled the hearty scent of roasting lamb, one of his favorite meals. He hadn't had fresh lamb in months, and this time he didn't have to chase it down and kill it himself. He preferred his meat bloody and raw during the full moon, but cooked meat would keep his urges at bay. At least it would until the sun set. Then he had to make like Cinderella and take his pumpkin coach as far away from Charlotte as possible.

They sat on her living room couch. She uncorked the wine and poured two glasses. "Let's have a toast," she said as she held up her glass. Sam did in kind. "To good friends."

"I'll drink to that. To good friends, it is."

They tapped their glasses together and drank. The tartness of the wine awakened his taste buds, which were much more sensitive to the nuances of food when the full moon hung high in the sky. He savored mouth-puckering purple grapes and a hint of blackberry. There was also a touch of chocolate essence in the drink. The wine had just enough kick to calm his nerves, but not enough to untie his knotted tongue.

What am I going to say to her? I'd better think of something before I look even more stupid than I feel.

Where was the suave and debonair Sam who was so accustomed to situations like this? Had he never before invested much emotion in a relationship with a woman? Why was Charlotte so important to him? He'd already had sex with her several times, but tonight was different. With any other woman who interested him, he'd have turned on the charm and seduced her until she was in his bed within the next hour.

Not Charlotte. What made her so different that all his old tricks fell by the wayside? He knew what mattered about her. She had a level head on her shoulders. If he shifted in front of her, he knew she wouldn't completely freak out like other women in his past would have. She might be in shock at seeing him turn into more of a muscular, hairy beast than he already was, but she wouldn't lose her cool.

He needed someone like that in his corner.

He really didn't want her in bed this evening. He didn't want to ruin a good thing. He couldn't do that tonight anyway, not with the risk of shifting in front of her and scaring her to death.

"How's the wine?" Charlotte asked, interrupting his worrying.

"It's good. I like a good red."

She laughed and sipped. "I wouldn't call it a good red. More like it was a good week."

It was Sam's turn to laugh, and it was full of warmth and joy. Leave it to Charlotte to catch him off guard to alleviate the butterflies in his stomach. "I've always loved your sense of humor. You brighten up any room you're in. Lina isn't that much different, but she's quieter."

"Don't be fooled. She's just as wicked as I am." Charlotte smiled at him, her eyes dancing with mischief. "Which reminds me, how did you and Grant meet?"

He knew better than to tell her the truth, so he varnished his story a bit as he always did when anyone asked about his love life. "Grant and I met at a concert. He dropped his booze, and I shared mine with him. We've been together ever since." They'd actually met at a strip club, but he was too embarrassed to tell her that. The concert was a week later.

"Cool. I love concerts. Who did you see?"

Quick, think fast. He couldn't tell her it was at Woodstock because she'd wonder why he looked so young. "Oh, one of those reunion concerts. Santana. The Dead. CCR."

She laughed. "Which one? Make up your mind."

Sam's heart raced in his throat. He'd had this conversation a million times, but for some reason having it with Charlotte gave him a scorching case of the heebie-jeebies. "Santana. We went to a lot of concerts that summer. Later we found road crew work and got to see lots of bands for free. Front row and wing seats. Couldn't get much better than that."

"Wow, what I would give to see the Stones up close."

"Been there, done that."

As they talked, Sam relaxed. He wouldn't reveal his big

secret to Charlotte before he was ready. Despite his ease with her, he continued to stumble over his words. However, the wine loosened his tongue. He raved about Grant and repeatedly stated how much he loved him. Yes, they had an open relationship, and Charlotte has been one of their more memorable and favorite partners. She beamed at this, and her expression made him stammer even more. Why was he acting like a smitten grade school kid? Charlotte was comfortable, like a favored soft blanket, but she also set a fire in his loins unlike any woman before her.

He wanted to impress her. He rarely wanted to impress anyone.

As he relaxed, his appetite came roaring back with a vengeance. With his nervousness behind him, he followed Charlotte to her lovely and cozy dining room for their evening meal.

Dinner was as delicious as he expected it would be. Savory rare lamb filled his belly, reducing his urge to shift and feed. As they ate and chatted, time flew by quickly. He didn't even bother to check his watch. As the night wore on, he relaxed and enjoyed himself. Watching her eat, he felt a pang of hope. He needed her.

A quick glance at his watch told him it was only seven-thirty. He collected vintage watches, and tonight he wore a classic wind-up Timex. Plenty of time before the full moon appeared in the sky. He could enjoy his date with Charlotte without worry.

Once they finished their meal, she put on some trance music and joined him on the couch. Having drunk the wine he'd brought with their meal, she brought out a bottle of shiraz and poured two glasses. Sated with wine, drink, and good company, he settled back in the comfort of the couch and relaxed.

"I'm glad you asked me over for dinner," Sam said. "I wanted to spend some time alone with you, but I wasn't sure how to ask."

Was she blushing? Confident and down-to-earth Charlotte was as rosy as the shiraz she drank. "Well, I wanted to get to know you better for some time now. It just took me this long to ask you to come over."

"So, this is a date."

She turned from him and bit her lip. Sam's heart lurched a few beats. She was shy. He never would have guessed. "Yes, I suppose it is." Her voice quivered. She lowered her head, stammered something he couldn't understand, then raised her head to reveal a soft blush covering her cheeks. How endearing! This was a side of Charlotte he had never seen before. He doubted many people had seen this side of the enigmatic woman.

"I like our evening so far." He suddenly clammed up. Every pick-up line and mode of conversation left his head. Tongue-tied, he froze, not knowing what to say. Instead of speaking, he listened to the trippy beat of the music.

"I'm not usually so speechless," she whispered.

"Neither am I."

"I guess I'm nervous. I haven't been on a date in a very long time." She fidgeted in her seat. "Lina and I have an open relationship, but I'm very picky about my lovers. I have played the field, especially with this troupe, but I'm much more prudish than I let on."

He pulled away from her and stared at her face. "You're kidding, aren't you?"

She gave him a wan smile and shrugged her shoulders. "I usually don't run into men interested in getting to know me better. You're a refreshing change. So are Grant and Luke."

He warmed to her even more, wanting to draw her out of her shell. Beneath the hard and brash exterior, she was actually a shy and sensitive woman. She trusted him enough to see her at her most vulnerable.

"Most men want to get in my pants, and that's it. Part of it's the way I look. I guess it's the way I come across, too. I can be quite . . .brusque. That's just a front. I'm not as confident as I look. I've been burned quite a few times."

"Why do you keep going after people in the troupe?"

"I keep hoping the next one will be different. Lina has been a Godsend. I don't know what I'd do without her. We're looking for a third, though, and we're having trouble finding one."

"I had no idea. I thought you could have any guy you wanted." Sam smiled. "Or any woman."

She laughed. "Yeah, all the rumors you heard are true. Like I said, Lina and I have been looking for a third, but we haven't found one yet. I'm negotiable if the right person comes along." She grinned. "Or a fourth. A four-person ménage suits us well."

The good news rang like a song in his ears. He and Grant could satisfy them. The more they talked, the more he liked Charlotte. She opened herself up to him. If only he could do the same with her, but it was far too soon.

He wished he had more time to talk to her, to get to know her better. Time was a luxury. "You never know who the right person may be. You'll probably find him when you least expect it." He smiled again. "Or her."

"I hope he's right in my backyard." She stared directly into his eyes as she spoke. Her meaning was clear. Maybe they could make a go of it. They talked and teased each other often enough when striking sets. With ease he put his arm around her, and she responded to his touch by leaning her head against his chest. He pressed his face into her long, black hair, smelling the ocean scent of her shampoo in her tresses. He closed his eyes, taking in every tantalizing sensation he could muster from her, the curve of her body against his, the smell of her perfume, the feel of her small hands on his waist. If only he could hold her like this forever. That would be heavenly.

He opened his eyes and looked out the window. To his horror, he saw the full moon blazing amid shifting clouds. Storm clouds filled the sky. He hadn't expected rain. The darkening sky smelled of ozone. He looked at his watch.

It said seven-thirty. His watch had stopped.

He pulled away from her. "What time is it?"

"It's nine-thirty. Is something wrong?"

Hackles on the back of his neck stood on end. His skin tingled. Canine teeth slowly lengthened, and he felt their tips against his sensitive tongue. He tried to hold back the shifting, but the urge was too strong. Panicking, he looked for a fast way out.

"I have to go," He groaned as he rose too quickly. The room spun.

I have to get out of here. If I shift any more than this, I'll hurt her.

"Are you okay? You don't look so hot."

"I-I don't think I'm over that flu I had last week. I feel sick. It's not you. It's me. I had a wonderful time, but I really should go." The longer he talked, the deeper his voice became. He glanced at Charlotte. Her skin glowed with a radiance of the living creature she was. Her heartbeat boomed in his ears. He smelled her blood. He wanted her. He wanted to taste her, to consume her. Terrified, he turned and headed for her front door.

"I'm so sorry, Charlotte. I'm not good company tonight," He said, facing away from her. When her hand alighted on his back, all his nerve endings jumped at her touch. He resisted turning toward her because he knew to do so would mean he'd attack her.

"Go home and get some rest."

The dejection and disappointment in her voice saddened him. His heart ached for her. He wished he could make things better but now was not the time. Damn his curse.

"Make sure you call in tomorrow, so you don't get

docked."

"I'll do that. See you soon." He raced out the front door and headed for his car. Rain poured down, masking the change his body was going through as he ran down her driveway. By the time he sat in his car, his shoulders had already torn through his t-shirt and jacket. His hips threatened to rip his jeans but thankfully they had lots of give. He drove away under the cover of a welcome rainstorm. By the time he made it home, his transformation was nearly complete.

CHAPTER ELEVEN

A ction (n): Action is called when filming to signal the be-
ginning of a take.
Action (n): Scoring sexually.

While Sam spent time in Charlotte's company, Grant watched the dancers from the wings as he set up light trees. Luke had pointed out Willow, Cheyenne, and Melissa before he jetéed onto the stage. Melissa's raven hair and deep-set dark eyes disqualified her from being the shifter. Plus, she seemed very comfortable with her colleagues, something he doubted he'd see from his mysterious kindred. No, his enigmatic wolf would be awkward, timid, and a loner. She'd be very much like him, except that he had long ago blended in well with the people he lived and worked with. Her? Not so much.

Cheyenne warmed up on the stage a few yards in front of him. She sat with her legs outstretched ahead of her, stretching from one side to the other, alone, but she seemed much too comfortable in her body. She smiled and waved as dancers and crew meandered across the stage. A young male dancer Grant did not know came by with a small cup of steaming brew for her. Grant assumed it was coffee until he saw the string and label hanging from the mug. Cheyenne liked her chamomile tea piping hot.

When Willow crossed the stage, Grant knew immediately she was who he was looking for. Her flaming red hair was tied in a French braid. The grey leotard hugged her tiny frame. Small and delicate in stature, she couldn't have stood more than five foot two. A few dancers walked past her without speaking to her. As she blended into the background, he understood why he had never before noticed her. This woman did not want to be seen. She stretched in a private space of her own, all others unwelcome unless she allowed them in, and he suspected that was not often.

With grace that seemed effortless, she rose to her feet and wandered about the stage as if looking for someone. She spoke to a couple of crew members, who to his surprise pointed in his direction. Willow nodded, but rather than approach him, she walked to the side of the stage opposite him, pointedly refusing to look at him.

He and Sam had given her their names the night before. She was scoping him out. She probably worried he would give away her secret. He had to let her know he would never do such a thing, but he feared approaching her directly lest he scare her away. How far could she go, since she was here to rehearse? What was she going to do, hide behind craft services?

Running low on electrical tape, he wandered across the stage to a road crew box and grabbed a new roll. Willow had glanced to the wings where he had been only moments before, and she seemed rattled when she couldn't find him. She looked from right to left, becoming more flustered as she lost track of him. The poor woman trembled in her toe shoes.

"If you're looking for me, I'm right behind you," Grant said.

Willow whirled around on one toe, a move so graceful she took his breath away. Even ruffled she moved like a zephyr.

"I wasn't looking for you."

"Yes, you were. You've been looking for me since last night in the woods."

She flushed. "I have no idea what you're talking about."

He took a step toward her. She took a step back.

"I'm not going to hurt you. Neither is Sam. He's my partner. We want to help you."

She turned away from him. "I don't know what you're talking about."

Taking a chance, he rested one hand on her shoulder. She froze, and he wondered if he had taken a step too far in touching her. Her body shivered beneath his palm. She wore her fear like a cloak.

"You can't help me." He heard the dejection in her voice and wanted to do anything he could to comfort her.

"You're not alone, Willow. Sam and I can help you. So can Luke."

She turned toward him and stared at him with big, soulful hazel eyes. "Luke? How? I've never seen him in the woods."

"You may have seen him, but you didn't realize it. He's a shifter too, but he's not a wolf."

She paused, taking in his words. Rocking back and forth on her toes in a soothing motion, she narrowed her eyes as she contemplated what he told her. "How do you know you have the right woman? How do you know I won't go right up to those hunters tonight and set them on all three of you?"

"Because you would put yourself in danger in doing that."

"How do you know that's not exactly what I want, since it'll put me out of my misery?"

She had a point. If she had lost her will to live, which he feared, she would become reckless. One mistake and she could be felled very quickly. He had to convince her that she had friends in her corner who could not only help her but support her.

"What can I do to help you trust me?"

She stared at him again, her eyes shining with unfallen tears. Hers was the most soul-wrenching stare he had ever seen, and it cut him to the core.

"I'd like to trust you, but I'd be taking a huge chance. I'm not a risk taker. You seem like a nice guy. I don't know enough decent people, but you'd be better off not knowing me well."

"Let me be the judge of that. I've gone through what you're going through, and I can help. So can Luke and Sam."

"I don't know if anyone can help me. I trusted someone in Vegas, and he nearly got me killed. I trust no one."

"If you continue to feel that way, you'll end up dead."

"I'm willing to take that risk." She turned away from him and took a few steps onto the stage.

"Willow, wait." He moved toward her. She stopped. "Think about it, that's all I ask. I'm here when you need me." He said *when* rather than *if*, hoping she noticed the difference. "Sam's off today, but he'll be here tomorrow. Luke's on tonight. Talk to us. We can help you, but only if you ask."

She paused for what seemed like hours. "I'll think about it."

"Good. Maybe we can meet later, after rehearsal. Luke and I will be at the Black Horse."

"Maybe." She ran away before he could respond.

Grant sat in the Black Horse with Luke after rehearsal, facing the door, hoping to see Willow walk in any second. Was she too shy to hang out with them? The poor girl was so shy — more so than Lina, but Lina at least had that sexy teasing streak that made up for her shyness. Each time the door opened, Grant's heart skipped a beat, but he was disappointed to see hunters and families coming in for a few drinks and a late-night meal.

"If I didn't know better, I'd think you were ignoring me." Luke pretended to pout, but he couldn't hold the expression for longer than a few seconds without breaking out in a smile.

"Are you expecting Sam? I thought he'd be here with us to-night."

"No, he's at Charlotte's. On a date. They're having dinner tonight."

"I like her. She has spirit. Quick-witted, too. Nothing gets past her."

My shifting gets past her, thank God. "Not much does, at any rate. Actually, I'm waiting for Willow."

"Willow? Miss *I'm so shy I come across as stuck-up* Willow?"

"She doesn't seem stuck-up to me."

"The other dancers don't associate much with her because they think she thinks she's too good for them. I know it's not true, and I've said so, but getting Willow to talk is futile."

"I got her to talk a little bit, mainly because I wouldn't let her get away with her aloof act with me."

"I hope she joins us. I don't know her at all except in pass-ing."

To Grant's delight. Willow walked through the door. The tiny dancer looked ridiculously small in her overstuffed coat. Grant waved until he caught her attention, and she acknowl-edged him by giving him a great big face-lighting smile. If only she smiled like that more often, the other dancers wouldn't feel so put-off by her.

Willow approached their table, then took a chair. "I'm glad you waited for me. I hope I'm not too late."

"You're not late at all," Grant said.

"Good. I'm famished."

At first she said little, preferring to pick at a bowl of chili in silence and observe a group of rowdies paying darts. Grant ordered a pitcher of ale. Before long, with a little beer inside her, Willow opened up. She even seemed to enjoy herself.

"You two could pass for twins." Willow stared at Grant and Luke, doe-eyed with amazement.

Grant laughed, happy she'd relaxed enough to finally join

the conversation after five minutes of awkward silence on her part. "You're not telling us something we don't already know."

They sat in a cozy window booth, far from the drunken revelers who had been hunting all day but came up with nothing. Since they'd had an early start that day, rehearsal had finished by dinnertime, and Grant was so hungry he wolfed down much of his shepherd's pie. He was delighted Willow had chosen to join him and Luke. The longer they talked, the more she relaxed. She even smiled a few times. They had plenty of time before the full moon rose, so they could chill and chat a bit after work hours.

Despite a workout of a day, she picked at her food. She was only partly into her third month of turning, so her lack of appetite shouldn't have come as that much of a surprise.

"How can you possibly eat that with me sitting right next to you? I should be insulted." Luke said to Grant.

Grant smiled, enjoying the teasing. He dipped into his shepherd's pie and forked a piece of meat. "I'm eating venison in your honor. It's quite good, too. Want some?"

"Are you kidding? I'm not into cannibalism." Luke put on a sorrowful and insulted look, but one gaze into his dancing eyes told Grant he wasn't serious.

"I thought the only shifters were werewolves," Willow said.

"There are all kinds," Luke said. "I was born this way. I also have more control over my shifting into buck form, something Grant and Sam lack."

"Buck?" Willows eyes became as round as the full moon. She dropped her spoon into her chili, splashing it about the tabletop. "This has venison in it. I shouldn't have ordered it. I'm so sorry."

Luke patted her hand, picked up her spoon, and handed it to her. "It's okay. Nobody I'm related to, anyway. You eat.

You need your strength."

"Grant, you weren't born a shifter?" she asked.

"Nope, he wasn't." Luke interrupted Grant before he could speak. "Grant is a made man."

Grant told Willow his story, down to the last pilsner he had as a mortal human. She sat transfixed, spoon poised to her mouth, listening intently to every word.

"I know exactly what you're going through, Willow." Grant said. "Like you, my first time changing was alone in the woods without anyone to guide me. I was scared out of my wits. I hid in a lake until I got control of myself the next morning. It's not easy doing what I do—and what Sam does—but it's much easier to take if you have people in your corner."

"You're in my corner?" She sounded hopeful, as if her wariness was fading.

"Yes. We've never mentored anyone before, but we'll do it if you're interested." He held his breath, hoping to convince her to trust him.

"How come I've never seen you shift completely?" She narrowed her eyes with disbelief, and Grant bit his tongue to keep from voicing his disappointment. *No, just keep her talking and convince her you're trustworthy with your words.*

"Sam and I drink this concoction made from monkshood and rye. Neither of us can stomach it much, but it does help us maintain control. I won't completely shift as long as I drink it." He pulled a large flask from his waist. "Want to try it?"

She eyed it warily. "No. I don't drink hard liquor."

Grant didn't blame her. "It'll help. Trust me. You'll sing my praises the first time you try it, even if you gag the whole time you're swallowing it."

She paused, staring at the flask as if he held a large rattlesnake in his hand. "It'll really help?"

"Yes."

"It will. I've seen what it can do," Luke said. "It really does work. Something that tastes that vile must work."

She sat her spoon in her chili and cocked her head at him. "Okay. May I have a sip of it?"

"Sure. Try it. Just be warned. It tastes like outhouse water."

"Thanks. Just what I need." She took the flask and opened it, leaning over to take a good whiff. Her nose curled. "Oh, God, that's awful, and you expect me to drink this?"

"Yup." Luke and Grant said in unison.

She took a sip, and her face immediately twisted in disgust. "Ew, God, that's dreadful, but it really helps?"

"Yes. Try a bit more of it. It grows on you," Grant said.

"Like mold," Luke said.

She laughed. Not only was it a pleasant sound, her laugh softened the contours of her face, giving her a less desperate look. She had nearly relaxed completely, pleasing Grant very much. Little by little, he was winning her over.

Taking a deep breath, she held up the flask. "Bottoms up." She tilted her head back as she placed the flask's opening against her lips and guzzled a huge swallow of the stuff. After coughing until her face turned red, she handed the flask back to Grant.

"It's bad, but not so bad that I can't get used to it."

"It's easy to make. I'll give you the recipe." Grant said. "Make sure you drink it tonight before the moon rises. It'll help. You'll have better control of yourself."

She lowered her head so he couldn't see her face. At first, he thought she was going to be sick from the drink, but when she lifted her head, her eyes shined bright with tears. "What can I do to thank you both? I don't even know you, and you're being so good to me." She wiped her face with her napkin and gave them a hesitant and self-conscious laugh. "I don't normally carry on like this. Most of the time no one will have anything to do with me."

I got her. Now that she's in my corner, I can tend to her. Thrilled at the prospect of training a newbie, Grant warmed to his new role as mentor. He felt sage and confident he could direct Willow in the right direction for her life.

"We're not just anyone. Trust us." Luke said. "We have much in common, and we should stick together. In addition to dance and theater, I believe we have movies in common."

"As long as you don't ask her to watch *The Brotherhood of the Wolf*." Grant rolled his eyes.

"I love that movie. Even now. I never get tired of it," she said.

"What is it with werewolves and shifter movies?" Grant smiled at her, and when she smiled back at him, creasing laugh lines around her eyes, his heart warmed. He'd never taken on a mentee beside Sam, and Sam was different because he was also Grant's lover. Grant viewed Willow as his lost little sister who needed his help. He suspected Luke and Sam saw her the same way. She was so small and vulnerable, afraid but friendly at the same time. He felt a strong urge to protect her.

"You changed in Vegas a few months back?" Grant asked.

"Yes. I'd just started dating a guy in the crew. He was a sound assistant. We'd been practicing matching my moves to the music when he asked me out."

"You were lead dancer?" Luke asked.

"No. Secondary lead. There were three of us, and I was having trouble with a couple of moves. Brian helped me with my solo bit. We must have rehearsed all afternoon."

"How long did you date before he changed you?"

"About three weeks. I was really into him, too. I don't normally go for the people I work with, because I've had a few bad breakups. Working with people you've ended it with isn't a lot of fun."

"I know." Luke said. "I made that mistake a few times myself."

"How do you and Sam pull it off?" Willow asked Grant.

"We met before we started doing crew work. Plus, being Lycan created an intense bond between us."

"It didn't between Brian and me. Not long after he turned me, he vanished. I heard he left to follow another road show. He didn't even say goodbye. There I was, in an unfamiliar place, smack in the middle of the desert, and I had no one to guide me."

"What happened the first time you shifted?"

"It was shortly before he left. I hid in the desert and lived on wildlife. Luckily there were some tall cactus, so I was able to hide well enough. I begged Brian to help me, but he ignored me. Gave me the cold shoulder immediately. He blamed me for what happened, saying I shouldn't have seduced him on the full moon because he can't control himself."

"This Brian sounds like a dick," Luke said.

"He was. I wanted out of Vegas once I changed. I saw this show in the trade papers and auditioned. Got in on the first try." She smiled. "Shifting has given me more energy and I'm more limber. It's actually improved my dancing."

"How did you end up going from a leading role to chorus?" Grant asked.

"I took a pay cut to get the part. I didn't care. I needed to get as far away from there as fast as I could. Everything reminded me of Brian. The neon lights. A Cirque. We saw a show together. I loved it, but I can't go to the circus anymore because it brings back such painful memories. I can't even play blackjack because it reminds me too much of him. At least I often won. That used to piss him off. He lost money, and I made it."

"It's not too expensive here, so you're in luck," Luke said. "I could put in a good word for you if you're still up for a leading role. There's a rumor one of the lead female dancers is leaving. If it's true, I'll vouch for you. I've watched you dance. You have the moves."

She clapped her hands to her mouth, eyes bright with gratitude. She picked up a napkin and shredded it into tiny pieces. "That's very kind of you. I could use the money. I feel the pain of the pay cut, but I really needed to get out of there. I've always wanted to visit the Pacific Northwest, and here I am. Thanks, if you're able to speak up on my behalf." By the time she stopped chattering, a mound of torn napkin had grown in front of her.

Grant took her hands in his and gave them a squeeze. "You don't have to be so nervous in front of us."

"I don't know what you mean."

"You just made mincemeat of that napkin."

She laughed. "Oh, that. Bad habit I've had since I was a kid. I chew my nails, too. Never been able to break either habit."

She'd admitted she was the nervous sort. What could Grant do to make her feel more comfortable?

"How about we meet here most nights after rehearsal? Make it a tradition until the show ends." He liked the idea very much. Being a nomad, he had to come up with creative ways to create consistency in his life. Meeting with the same people after rehearsal was one way to establish a pleasant routine.

"I like that idea. Thanks. No one ever asked me to join them before," Willow said.

"That's not completely true," Luke said. "When we first started the tour some, of the dancers asked you to join them for drinks, but you refused."

She sighed, blushing until her cheeks turned bright pink. "Yeah, that's true. I'm usually too scared to join others because I don't know what to say. I'm afraid I'll come across looking like an idiot."

Grant smiled. "You don't look like an idiot to me."

"Me, neither," Luke said.

"Well, I'll make a point of being here when you two are."

"It's also the full moon." Grant reminded her. "Time for shifting. You don't have to do it alone."

"Thank you. It's funny, but when I'm not shifting it's like it's so far away and so foreign to me, I can't imagine doing it. Then when it happens, I panic."

"That's normal," Grant said. "When you shift tonight, make a point of getting to the quarry. There's a cave there you can hide in. Find me, Sam, and Luke, and we'll protect you. Us shifters must stick together, especially with all those ya-hoos running around with rifles."

"Yes, I wondered about that. To think I wanted to die. I don't feel so alone anymore."

"Just remember to find us right before you feel shifting coming on. We'll watch each other's backs."

"I'll do that. Thank you very much. I've never had friends before. Not really. I feel comfortable with you guys. I'm talking non-stop. I never talk."

Her smile warmed Grant's heart. Willow wasn't aloof at all. The other dancers were wrong about her. She was very sweet and considerate. Vulnerable. She didn't make friends easily, but Grant had taken to her not long after she opened up to him and Luke. She trusted them enough to both confide in them and seek them out the next time she shifted. He only hoped things went well for her.

"Well, I have to go because I'm tired."

"Oh, wait." Grant pulled a sheet of paper and a pen out of his pocket and scribbled on it. "These are the ingredients and recipe for our monkshood rye mix. You can find monkshood downtown in that health food store on Main. You know, the one across from the police station?"

"Yup, I know it. Thank you again. I'll mix some of this stuff up tonight."

"Just remember to avoid the hiking and bike paths in the woods. Too many people. You'd be in danger there," Grant said. "How do you feel now?"

"Not too bad. A bit wonky, but I can control it for now. I do feel a need to run, though."

"That's common. The urge comes and goes. Just stay off the common paths."

"If you do shift there, I can find you and guide you out." Luke said. "You'll know me when you see me. I'm the talking deer," He grinned.

Willow thanked them for the third time and walked for the door. Grant watched her as she crossed the room. She seemed so small compared to the burly drunks and the boisterous regulars. They'd tear her to bits if they knew what she was. He'd do everything in his power to keep the nasties at bay. Anything to protect his new adopted little sister.

CHAPTER TWELVE

Chase (v): A sequence of light changes that make it look as if the lights are moving. Also known as chase lights.
Chase (v): To pursue for the purpose of sexual gratification

Sam awakened the next morning feeling like a mountain after a plane had crashed into it. His ears buzzed, and his skin hurt. Sunlight flooded the room, making him squint so hard he buried his head beneath the blankets. His head pounded, and the last thing he wanted to do was crawl out of bed.

The door opened, and Grant came in with the delicious smell of fresh coffee floating about him. He carried a tray laden with breakfast. Dressed in only a pair of loose-fitting sweatpants, his powerful body excited Sam, who wanted to run his hands over that broad, hairy chest. Heady scents of juniper and rosemary from Grant's shower gel floated around Sam like a cloud. With a deep breath, he inhaled, taking in the crisp smell. He felt the stirrings of desire, knowing a romp would ease his headache very quickly.

"Hi, lover." Grant sat the tray in front of Sam and sat next to him.

"I feel horrible. My head is throbbing." Sam said as he gripped the sides of his head with both hands.

"You had a rough time last night. I found you naked on the living room rug when I got home at midnight. I had to drag you to bed. You're not the lightest person on earth."

"I was on the rug?"

"You don't remember?"

"Nope."

"You went to Charlotte's last night. Shifting in front of her wasn't a smart idea."

"I didn't do it on purpose. My watched stopped."

"I know. You told me. I told you before to get a digital watch, but you won't listen to me." Grant said as he sat the tray on the bed.

"Did I kill anyone, get into any fights, scare Charlotte to death?"

"No, no, and no," Grant said. He skewered some scrambled eggs and held the fork out to Sam. "Here, eat. You need your strength. You didn't drink the rye mix, did you?"

"I didn't think I'd need it. I drank a good bit of it here before I left. It got dark fast, and I thought I'd be home before the moon rose, but my watch stopped. Charlotte didn't see me shift. I hope." He took the fork and helped himself to his food.

"No. She called about an hour ago. She's worried about you. You bolted. She thinks you're mad at her."

"Not a chance. I started shifting in front of her, and I had to get out."

"Call her. She's very confused."

"I know." Sam sipped his coffee. "I've been thinking . . . if we're going to get closer to Charlotte and Lina, we're going to have to spill the beans about what we really are."

"We could always show them *The Howling* and say, you know, not all werewolves are like that," Grant said with a twinkle in his eye.

"I thought you didn't like werewolf movies?"

"I was humoring you," Grant said with a smirk. "We'll eventually have to tell them the truth, but can we trust them?"

"I think we can, but how do we bring it up? It's not like they'll believe a word we say if we tell them we're Lycan.

They'll just accuse us of pulling another one of our practical jokes."

"You shift when you're horny. Charlotte makes you horny. Problem solved."

"I can't help it. Have you looked at her tits lately? They defy gravity. Now I can't stop seeing them in my mind's eye. Shifting might work if I'm horny enough, which shouldn't be a problem at all, but wouldn't she be too shocked? I'm afraid she'll go shrieking away from us and tell everyone."

"Who would believe her?"

"Those hunters, for one."

"I do like the idea of shifting in front of them, but maybe only a little. How about we take extra monkshood rye that night, then explain ourselves? We won't completely shift in front of them, so it won't be so shocking."

"Good idea. Maybe. I don't know. I'm so confused." Sam wriggled in bed and picked up his coffee mug. He took a sip and savored the taste of the magical brew as it flowed down his throat. "Talking about shifting while being horny is making me horny, and I need coffee. I hate Lycan hangovers."

"Ah, so you want sexy time? Coffee can wait. I have a better hangover remedy. You need tending to."

Sam knitted his brows in confusion as Grant took the coffee mug from his hand and placed it on the breakfast tray. Grant then picked up the tray and sat it on a table next to the bed.

When he turned to Sam, he lowered the covers to reveal Sam's naked body. Sam's erection bobbed in the air, begging to be man-handled.

"What's this I see? You might be a bit worse for wear this morning, but your equipment seems to be working properly." Grant gripped Sam's penis, sliding his palm down until he fisted at the base, eliciting a deep groan from Sam. "You like that?"

"Mmmm."

"How about you turn over and I care for you properly? Your headache will be gone in no time."

With one broad movement, Grant grabbed the comforter and top sheet and yanked them to the bottom of the bed. Sam turned onto his stomach. Sam always slept naked. He hated strangling in clothing when drifting into dreamland.

At the sight of Sam's lithe body, Grant felt the stirrings of desire. Since Sam felt a bit worse for wear this morning, Grant moved slowly. He grabbed a bottle of massage oil and squeezed it into his palms. The sharp tang of cinnamon slammed into his nose. He straddled Sam's legs and pressed his hands into Sam's lower back.

"Oh, God that feels good. I need it." He moaned. "I think I pulled something when I raced out of Charlotte's house."

"I'm going to pull something in a bit that will take your mind off sore muscles."

"I won't stop you."

Grant kneaded Sam's back on each side of his spine until his muscles warmed and softened. The massage oil warmed as he worked his magic, eliciting groans of pleasure from Sam. The stirring in his groin turned to a full-on erection, but he needed to warm Sam up first. As Grant's hands moved up Sam's body, he pressed his fingers into Sam's most sensitive areas, the places where he knew he hurt the most. Hauling lights and pushing road boxes left both of them in a perpetual state of dull pain that frequent massages alleviated. Grant homed in on those spots beneath Sam's shoulder blades, massaging in tight circles until those muscles loosened and relaxed.

He admired Sam's body, which was so much slimmer than his own. Smooth skin warmed beneath his palms, and the more Grant touched Sam, the more he wanted to thrust into him, but it was not yet the right moment. He stole periodic glances between Sam's legs to see his lover's own erection growing quickly. Sam's body soon surrendered beneath Grant's palms. He used the heels of his hands to push against Sam's shoulders, then gripped him with his fingers and thumbs to press the stiffness from tendons and muscles. Once Grant's thumbs pressed against the sides of Sam's neck, he moved on to more exciting endeavors.

He slathered oil on his hands and erection. Eager to get on with the best part of his massage, he kneaded Sam's ass cheeks until they turned pink. Then he inserted his slick index finger into Sam's anus up to one knuckle.

Sam groaned, as Grant expected him to. Grant moved his finger around in tight circles until Sam's sphincter relaxed enough for him to slide in all the way. Once Sam was completely relaxed, he pulled out, slathered his cock with oil, spread Sam's legs apart, then gently slid his hardness home as Sam hoisted himself to his knees.

Grant closed his eyes and enjoyed the tight, warm glove around his cock. Sam arched his back in ecstasy, moving slowly with Grant's rhythm. Both men soon matched their movements to each other, with Grant slamming faster and faster into Sam. He reached around and fisted Sam's thick tool, pumping it as he thrust harder and deeper into his ass. The sharpness of cinnamon mingled with the smell of Sam's warming skin. Sweat beaded on his back. Grant's labored breathing raced along with his throbbing heart. As his balls receded toward his body, he felt the familiar stirring of orgasm approaching. He tightened his grip on Sam's cock, which seemed to enlarge with every sweet stroke.

With a cry, Sam unloaded onto the sheets, his stomach, and Grant's hand. Overcome by his own orgasm, Grant spurted into Sam with each thrust. He continued thrusting until he grew limp and slid out. Sam collapsed on the bed, and Grant dropped right next to him.

"Headache's gone." Sam smiled.

"I knew it would be." Grant wrapped his arm around Sam, and both men dozed off.

When Grant awakened twenty minutes later, Sam had draped one arm over his torso, and he entwined his legs with Grant's.

Sam opened his eyes, blinking away sleep. "That was nice. Thank you for the pleasant surprise."

"I enjoyed it too, lover." He kissed Sam on the lips and sat up. "I love you very much, you know that?"

"I love you more," Sam said with a wink.

"You're such a tease." Grant stood up and stretched. "I'm starving. I'm always hungry after we get it on."

"Want me to join you?"

"No, you eat here. Make sure you're fully rested. You had a bit of a rough night." Grant returned the breakfast tray to Sam. "The food's probably cold by now, but I think that's worth the price you paid." He stroked Sam's bare shoulder. "I'll top off your coffee. You need to call Charlotte. She's worried."

"I'm sure she is." Sam reached for his phone and punched in Charlotte's number.

"I'll leave you to your breakfast. I'll be back with more coffee." Grant squeezed Sam's bicep and walked out of the room.

Sam swallowed a huge mouthful of coffee. He felt hung over. The rye mixture they drank not only prevented them from fully shifting, it also acted as a hangover remedy. A full shift sometimes left Sam with a pounding headache, sore muscles, and stiff joints. He could go without drinking alcohol and ending up hung over anyway.

After several rings, Charlotte answered her phone.

"Hello?"

"Charlotte, it's me, Sam."

"Are you okay?"

"I'm fine, although a bit strung out. I had a wonderful time last night. I didn't want you to think I ditched you. It was rude of me to run like that, but I felt terribly sick." It wasn't a lie. He *had* felt sick, so what he said wasn't far from the truth.

"You didn't look too great. As long as you're okay, that's all that matters." She snorted. "I hope the food didn't make you sick."

"Not a chance. That lamb was as tender as could be."

Grant walked in with a French press and poured coffee into Sam's cup. He squeezed Sam's arm, smiled, and left the room.

"Are you okay enough for Lina and me to come over tonight after we get off work? We could all hang out." She giggled. "I have another surprise for you."

"I love surprises. Sure, I'll be well enough for us to meet up tonight. Grant and I have the day off. Come on over right after your shift ends. We'll be home."

They rang off. A plate of eggs over easy, bacon, and sage sausage had Sam's name on it, and he ate with gusto. He finished his breakfast and carried his tray into the kitchen, where Grant sat drinking coffee. He set the tray on the kitchen counter and refilled his cup.

"I have more news." Grant said. "I met our intrepid shifter last night."

Sam whirled around. "Who is it? Is she a dancer?"

"Yes, and her name is Willow. Luke pointed her out to me. Little red head in a grey leotard."

Sam shook his head. "She doesn't sound familiar."

"That's no surprise. She's a bit of a wallflower. Blends into the background so no one notices her. I confronted her and told her about us and Luke. She was petrified."

"Who can blame her? What's she like?"

"She's scared, very depressed, and lonely. She also said someone turned her in Vegas, someone she'd trusted, so she's very gun-shy."

"She won't talk to us?"

"She will. She sure did last night. She has trouble trusting people, but I think Luke and I made a huge impression on her."

"Can't say I blame her. If I didn't have you, I'd be a nutcase by now." Sam sipped his coffee and closed his eyes, the brew working its magic. "What do we do with her?"

"We try to keep her out of harm's way tonight. I gave her some monkshood rye so she can control her shifting a bit. Taught her how to make it herself."

"How do we find her?" Sam asked.

"That shouldn't be hard. Luke and I met with her at the Black Horse last night. We ate venison in front of him."

"How rude."

"He thought it was amusing."

"So how are we meeting with her?"

"She said she'd like to hang out with us. I'm sure we'll run into her at the Black Horse. Then we can talk her into spending the night with us, so she isn't alone."

"Sounds like a plan."

"Charlotte and Lina are coming over later. Charlotte has a surprise for us," Grant said. "You know Charlotte and her little games. Whatever it is she's up to, it's bound to be good."

"I could use a bit of relaxation. Let's just hope it's something fun and sexy."

"Knowing Charlotte, that's exactly what it is."

CHAPTER THIRTEEN

Climax (n): The point in a play when the plot reaches a crisis point.
Climax (v): To reach orgasm

Sam basked in the afterglow of his and Grant's lovemaking long into the late afternoon. He and Grant puttered about their house, cleaned up, made love again, showered together, and watched a movie. Not long after a light dinner, the doorbell rang.

Charlotte, Lina, and Luke stood in the doorway, the three of them grinning like they had some big secret they were itching to share with the boys.

"I hope you don't mind we dragged Luke along," Charlotte said.

"Not at all," Sam said. "C'mon in. Beer's in the fridge. Help yourselves."

Grant turned on some trippy trance music, getting everyone in that partying mood. Grant sat out plates filled with nibbles—brie, apple slices, broccoli, onion dip, carrots. Rabbit food. After a few drinks and some spirited conversation, Charlotte raised her hand, asking for everyone's attention.

"I want to play a game. Are you in the mood for something sexy?"

"I'm always in the mood," Sam said.

"Yes, he is. He proved it once already today," Grant said with a grin.

"TMI! TMI!" Lina waved her hands in front of her face. "At least you're good to go."

Charlotte pulled a pair of dice out of a velvet drawstring bag and rolled them in her palm. They were large. Sam could easily read the writing on them. She shoved the empty bag into her back pocket.

"What do you say we play with my Sex Dice?" Charlotte asked.

"What are Sex Dice?" Luke asked, looking so open and naïve Sam wanted to hug him.

"He's adorable." Charlotte brushed her fingers against Luke's arm, making Luke double-take at her bold gesture.

The thrill of the chase coursed through Sam. He glanced at Grant, who winked at him. Grant must have been thinking the same thing Sam thought-they were going to get very lucky tonight many times over.

Charlotte continued. "In Sex Dice we shake the dice and do whatever they tell us to do. One die says what to do, and the other die says to whom to do it."

Luke reached for the dice in Charlotte's hand, but Lina slapped him away. That was the second time in only a few days that she slapped his hand away. Stirrings of excitement rippled up and down Sam's spine.

She likes slapping. I could get into a little swat. The pain would do me good.

"No touching." Lina commanded. "I'd rather see your reaction the moment you have to remove your shirt or French kiss the person to your right."

Mirth filled Grant's voice. "Good thing we're bi, or that could be awkward."

"Or enticing." Charlotte nibbled brie from an apple slice. Melted cheese dripped from the corner of her mouth, and the tip of her tongue snatched it up before it could get away, making Sam's cock twitched with delight.

"Have you ever seen two women kiss?" Charlotte teased

Luke. "It's very exciting. Some of them love putting on a show for a straight male audience."

"Good thing we're not straight males. We get double the benefit," Grant said.

"Enough talk. Let's play. Everyone on the floor in a circle." Sam took the dice from Charlotte. The five of them sat on the floor with Sam against the couch and to his right Grant, then Lina, Luke, and Charlotte.

"I'll go first," He took a sip of his cognac and tossed the dice on the rug.

The dice read *Hug* and *Person to your right.*

"That's easy enough." Sam hugged Grant and nibbled his earlobe, then stuck his tongue in his ear.

"Hey, lover, the die said hug." Grant shivered. "That doesn't include giving me a bath. I'm making you stick to the rules."

"Party pooper."

"Oh, this party's just getting started." Grant grabbed the dice. "My turn." He tossed them on the rug.

The dice read *Remove article of clothing* and *Person across from you.*

"I will torment *all* of you." Grant crawled into Luke's lap and tugged at his tight t-shirt, but grinned until his dimples deepened. Instead of removing Luke's shirt to show off his amazing torso, he untied Luke's black sneaker, removed it, and sat it next to him. Laughing, he scooted backward on his ass until he once again sat next to Sam.

"Cock tease," Sam said, almost sad he hadn't put shoes and socks on to have them removed so sensually.

"Slut." Grant punched his fist against Sam's arm, bringing forth a pleasant ache that sent shivers to Sam's body.

Then Lina tossed the dice, getting *Kiss* and *Second person to the right.* She slunk across the rug on all fours like a cat in heat while Charlotte's palms moved down her arms, fingers lightly brushing the sides of her breasts.

Sam squirmed, making room in his pants for his growing cock.

Lina craned her neck until her lips pillowed Charlotte's. Tongues flicked, touching each other, then darting back into open mouths. Eyes at half-mast, Charlotte's dreamy expression invited no one else to partake in her sensuous kiss.

Sam resisted an urge to crawl to them and join in. He knew he wouldn't be welcomed. *Not yet, anyway.*

Charlotte's hands caressed Lina's pendulous breasts, lifting them and pinching her nipples.

Sam tightened his stomach, his arousal growing stronger. He couldn't take his eyes off their bald expression of lust. He wanted more.

Lina pulled away and smiled at Charlotte, who brushed her palms along Lina's outer thighs.

Sam fingered his collar, providing an escape for the heat rising from his body.

That woman's touch has raised the temperature at least ten degrees in here.

Sam pulled his t-shirt from his jeans, giving himself room to breathe.

"You're supposed to wait until the dice tell you to undress, lover," Grant pinched his arm.

Sam swatted his hand away. "It's hot in here. Mind if I turn on the air conditioning?"

"It's forty degrees outside. Sounds like you're overheating from all the excitement. It's Luke's turn." Charlotte gave him a trouble-making grin. "Maybe you'll get lucky."

Luke rolled the dice, and Sam hoped whatever came to pass, Luke would act out his lustful fantasies on him. He got his wish.

The dice read, *Remove article of clothing* and *From anyone.*

Luke looked around, obviously drawing out the agony of whom he would choose. He leaned toward Grant, then turned his body toward Sam. Crawling on all fours, he moved across the rug until he faced Sam. He fingered one belt loop of Sam's jeans.

"I want these off. Now."

Sam hoisted himself up onto his knees, unzipped his jeans, and started to pull them down when Luke grabbed his hands. Confused, Sam stared into those amazing emerald eyes, corners creasing as Luke smiled at him. Lust and amusement lurked in those green depths. Luke slipped his fingers around the waistband and lowered the jeans.

Sam's erection strained beneath his boxer briefs, begging to be released from its fabric prison. His balls felt heavy and tight from arousal. More than anything, he wished for the feel of Luke's hands around his cock and balls, caressing until he grew so rigid, he could cleave an oak tree.

Luke pressed the back of his hand against Sam's cock, which jumped and strained against Luke's hand, wanting more than the torture of promise. Sam grasped Luke by the shoulders and moaned in his ear.

"Reach inside. Hold me."

Luke's tongue flicked against Sam's earlobe, eliciting shivers of ecstasy up and down his spine. "No, not yet. Wait your turn. You might get lucky and get to play with me."

Disappointed but thrilled at his future prospects, Sam leaned back, and Luke pulled off his jeans. Dressed only in his t-shirt, boxer briefs he felt naked and exposed to his friends and lovers. He hoped Charlotte wouldn't take long on her turn. He wanted his chance to ravish Luke.

"Damn. That's not fair." Charlotte sulked when the dice ordered her to skip a turn. Regardless of the other die said, if one said miss a turn, it canceled out the other one. "Your turn, sweetie," Charlotte grinned as she handed the dice to Sam. "I hope you get lucky. I want to see you and Luke molest each other right in front of me."

"The thought *had* crossed my mind."

"You've been eye-fucking each other since you met," Lina said. "It's about time you got down to it here rather than behind the flats."

So she knew. Everyone knew. There were no secrets in stage crew.

Sam rolled the dice, and his heart thumped when he saw what the dice told him to do.

Choose two persons and *Remove an article of clothing.*

He placed one palm on Grant's thigh and held his arm out to Luke. "I choose the two of you."

He removed both men's jeans so quickly he didn't bother to leave them in a tidy folded pile on the floor behind him. They ended up tossed in the corner in a heap. He reached into Grant's boxer briefs and grasped his erect cock. Luke pulled off Grant's shirt and then his own. The two men turned to each other, lips meeting, parted slightly as tongues danced. The sight of his lover kissing a man who looked so much like him excited Sam to the point of bursting.

"I guess the game is over." Charlotte pulled Sam's t-shirt over his head from behind. Her bare breasts pressed against his back, hard nipples digging into his skin as she rubbed her breasts back and forth against his shoulder blades. Her fingers slipped around the waistband of his boxer briefs.

"What's in here?" she moaned in his ear.

Grant fisted Sam's cock. "My favorite toy."

Delicious sparks of excitement shot through Sam's groin. He leaned backward against Charlotte's twin pillows as Grant stroked, long and slow. Sam reached into Luke's shorts until his fingers wrapped around his cock. He closed his eyes and took in the feel of every bump and nub until he knew it by touch. When he gripped Grant's cock in his other hand, he knew he had both men exactly where he wanted them.

Lina's lovely face appeared over Grant's shoulder as she

pressed her lips against his throat, seeking the throbbing pulse.

How wonderful is it to savor four lovers at once? He'd never had so many lovers at his beck and call before.

Over-stimulated from all the hands and mouths caressing his body, Sam relaxed against Charlotte's breasts and stroked Luke and Grant, slowly and ever so gently. Both men grew hard in his palms as he stroked. He stroked in time with the beating of the pulse in Grant's throat. Grant's nipples had hardened as Lina sucked on his ear and ran her hands over his massive chest.

It doesn't get much better than this. Luke's and Grant's sweet cocks in my palms. The two sexiest women on the crew, and they're here massaging and kissing us.

Sam closed his eyes. Heat from Charlotte's body warmed his back. Her fingernails running down his skin sent shivers up and down his spine, making his cock jump in Luke's hand. He turned his head and buried his face in her hair. Seagrass and moss scent brought forth fond memories of distant oceans, waves churning above still, vibrant depths full of life.

Luke released Sam's cock, and Sam groaned in protest. When Luke's lips wrapped around the head of his cock, Sam's body tightened, a rigid bundle of sexual tension. His groaning took on the feral edge he feared.

He pressed his mouth against Charlotte's full, bee-stung lips mainly to shut himself up. Their softness brushed against him like a butterfly's wings. He slipped his tongue in her mouth. Orange's faint whisper rolled over his tongue, the promise of tropical ecstasy lingering within her mouth.

Then the change took over.

CHAPTER FOURTEEN

Thrust (n): Type of stage that juts into the house so that the audience is seated on at least two sides of the extension. Thrust (v): To penetrate, push forward, as in thrusting while enjoying sexual penetration.

Sam's arms grew, and his muscles flexed. Hair rumpled as it lengthened, falling in his face. Fingers elongated, and nails grew into sharp claws. He *wanted* to shift in front of Charlotte. His heart warmed to his pack of lovers, each one tending to him in his or her unique way. He didn't want to lose any of them.

That meant making roots. Could he stop moving from place to place with each tour? Could he talk Grant out of his wanderlust?

Liking and trusting Charlotte, he risked scaring her. Would she accept him? He and Grant had talked about shifting in front of her only a few hours earlier. Now was his chance to test her. He feared Lina would reject him if Charlotte did. How would she react?

Should I shift? It's not like I could completely stop it.

He couldn't let it get too far, or he'd get lose control. The last thing he wanted to do was hurt Charlotte.

Okay, shift only a little, enough to show what I really am.

He'd drunk enough of the monkshood rye concoction earlier in the day to help him maintain control.

Take a chance. Let them know your secret.

He fisted her hair, pulled her away and opened his eyes.

Charlotte screamed. She scooted away from him on her ass until she backed into Luke, who wrapped his arms around her.

Lina crawled away on all fours, anguished mewling emerged from her throat, her gaze flitting all over Sam's transforming body. She hid behind Luke and Charlotte, who struggled and pulled away as Sam reached out one hirsute arm.

"Don't be afraid. I won't hurt you," he said with a hoarse voice. Immediately, he cut his words short. He'd forgotten his voice lowered several octaves with shifting. When he shifted, his speech sounded like a serial killer pumped up on energy drinks.

"What the hell are you? What's wrong with your eyes? Let me out of here." Charlotte writhed in Luke's grip, but he wouldn't let her go.

I wanted her to see my eyes. They turn yellow when I shift. What a shock.

"Calm down, Charlotte. He wouldn't have shifted in front of you if he didn't trust you," Grant said. "I'm the same as Sam. I just don't shift as badly when I get aroused. He does."

Lina cowered behind Luke, cheeks pale, a look of sheer terror on her lovely face. She didn't say a word. Sam thought she was so scared she was unable to speak.

Charlotte stopped struggling and glared at Sam, disbelief washing over her face. "What the hell *are* you two?"

"Three," Luke said. "I do it, too."

Charlotte whimpered in terror and tried to pull away, but Luke held fast. Lina found her voice and squealed a weak scream, but she didn't flee. Was it because she was too terrified to move or because her curiosity got the better of her?

Sam didn't approach either woman. He crossed his legs and continued talking in a low calm voice, hoping to put them at ease. First taking a few deep breaths, he spoke slowly as the coarseness in his voice subsided.

"I guess it's obvious enough what we are, although Luke turns into a fifteen-point buck that will be on someone's wall and dinner table if he isn't careful." Sam smiled, hoping his disarming grin would calm Charlotte and Lina, but it only scared them more. He remembered too late that his canine teeth grew very long — and sharp. "Oh, God, sorry about the teeth. I forgot how scary they look. I won't hurt you. None of us will. You told me you love adventure, Charlotte. Well, now you have it in spades."

"How come we never saw you do this before?" Lina asked. She peered from beyond Charlotte's shoulder, no longer as terrified but still wary.

"Because it wasn't the full moon. Now, it is."

She reached out one hand with a bit of hesitation and brushed it against his barrel-shaped chest. Her hands, normally large and thickly veined from years of rendering sets, looked tiny when compared to the size of his massive body, even when he shifted only partially. His pecs rose and fell as he breathed steadily, both to calm himself and to ward off further shifting.

"How long have you been like this?"

"A few decades. Grant's an old hand at it. He's been this way since 1931. Me? 1970. I was born in 1942."

"You saw the War."

"I saw several wars." Grant boasted.

"Aren't you special?" Charlotte quipped. Her laugh dissolved in a staccato beat of anxiety. "I'm having a hard time wrapping my head around this. I've seen a lot in my years, but nothing like this."

Sam scooted a little closer to her, but she held out her hands.

"No, not yet. I'm not taking this very well. Lina's scared, too. She's digging her fingernails into my shoulders. She's drawing blood."

Lina removed her hands. "Sorry about that. You're right. I don't know what to make of these two, er, three."

Realizing they weren't going to bolt after all, he relaxed, and his body began reverting into its human form.

"You're starting to look normal again," Charlotte said, "although you still have a massive amount of hair, and your eyes are still yellow."

"That'll take a while to level off. In a few hours, you won't even know I changed. I'll be back to my old, wonderful self." He grinned again, hoping his teeth had retracted along with the rest of his feral form.

"This will take some adjustment, but I'll manage. I take it you want your special talents to be kept a secret."

"Yes, please," the three men said at once and laughed.

"Tomorrow is the last night of the full moon, so I won't shift again until next month. No worries. I won't get much bigger again tonight. I promise."

Lina cocked an eyebrow. "Is *everything* bigger?" Despite her nervousness, her playfulness rubbed off on him. He scooted toward both women. Neither moved away, although they gaped at him. He took Lina's hand and lowered it to his boxer briefs.

"What do you think?"

She stroked his thick cock, which had become more rigid in all the excitement. The lustiest expression crossed her face, which was no mean feat, since Lina was *always* horny. She was simply much quieter about it than Charlotte. Without being asked, she tugged on his briefs until he slipped them off.

"Is this okay?" she asked.

"Of course it is."

Her fingers cradled his balls as she stroked him, up and down, flicking her thumb against his head to smear his precum over his smooth skin. She put her thumb in her mouth and sucked.

"Mmmmm. I want more," she said.

He stroked her hair. Charlotte leaned toward him, her gaze wandering to his erection, both women calmer than they were moments earlier.

"See?" Sam said. "I'm not as scary as you think."

"No, you're not." Charlotte said. "You're the same old Sam but with eyes that look like brass buttons."

"So?" Lina stroked his cock. "Does it taste different after you shift?"

"Why don't you find out for yourself?"

Her mouth and tongue felt smoother than Luke's. As she caressed his cock with her small, tight mouth, Grant rotated a finger around Sam's asshole until it relaxed. Once his finger slid inside, Sam felt another shifting coming on, but he resisted with more force. His cock grew in Lina's mouth as he lay on one side, Lina attacking him from the front and Grant from the back.

"It's bigger, and the pre-cum taste is stronger." Lina said, then went back to ministering to Sam's needs.

Charlotte whispered in Luke's ear, giggling and muffling her speech so Sam couldn't hear. Luke's hands found her huge breasts and kneaded them, one after the other.

"I want to see you shift. You're a buck?"

"Yes, but I'd rather not do it right now." Luke said. "I'm enjoying myself with you too much. One shifter in a day is more than enough."

"I supposed you're right. So, let's get on with our party."

Sam stared at her breasts. The sight of those twin globes, nipples hard and brick red, waiting for eager lips, made his cock jump in Lina's mouth.

"I have a great surprise for us. Be right back."

Charlotte hustled to the kitchen, delicious ass wriggling as she ran, her giggles floating in the air around them. Sam was very happy she'd calmed down. His fears were not entirely unfounded, but she seemed to have accepted him. With a sense of calm, he relaxed. Lina was going with the flow, too. The last thing he wanted to do was lose his two newest friends, especially Charlotte. Delighted that she'd accepted him despite his secret, he sighed with relief. His shoulders relaxed. His hair no longer stood on end.

Luke's lips stretched into a knowing smile as if he knew something Sam didn't.

Luke's cock bobbed in front of Sam's face. "How about you take care of me until she gets back?" he asked.

Lina removed her lips from Sam's cock and scooted to his right, giving Sam room to minister to Luke. Sam's lips caressed Luke's head slowly and gently, easing the cock deeper into his mouth. Luke fondled Sam's balls with one hand and fisted Sam's hair with the other, moving his head back and forth at a brisk pace.

Sam shut his eyes, Luke's heady scent surrounding him, his masculine heat warming his face as he stroked Luke with his mouth. Then leather tails brushed against Sam's back, the only warning before a loud *thwack* of a flogger stung his bare ass.

"I think it's time for a little whipping. You kept that secret from us ever since we met you." Charlotte traced the leather tails of the flogger over Sam's back. "What do you say to a little pain?"

CHAPTER FIFTEEN

Flogger (n): Strips of canvas attached to a handle. Crew members use this item prior to painting to dust flats or scenery.

Flogger (n): A type of whip used in BDSM practices.

Charlotte brandished the black suede flogger in one hand and fingered her left breast with the other. Humming as difficult to pin down as a cricket's chirping sounded around Sam. Then he saw it—the purple jelly butterfly strap-on clit teaser. Charlotte liked her sex toys.

"Caught your eye, didn't it?" She waved the flogger over her head as her body wove from side to side like a cobra about to attack its prey. "I love wearing this butterfly. It always gets a positive reaction, so I'm getting off just watching *you* get off."

Luke placed his hands on the sides of Sam's face and urged him to continue sucking. Sam nodded at Charlotte and closed his eyes. Salt and sour semen assaulted his taste buds. He inhaled the rugged musk of Luke's masculinity deeply into his lungs. Dozens of soft suede tails tickled his back as Charlotte drifted the flogger over his skin. She massaged his ass until his skin warmed and softened as she prepared him for a spanking he richly deserved. Then, without warning, she smacked him hard on the ass.

Thwack! His cock jumped in Lina's mouth. *If I'm not careful I'll come in seconds and ruin her pretty hair.*

"Do you deserve punishment because you didn't tell Lina and me your secret?" Charlotte poked one slender foot against his ribs. "I think you do, and for that you get this."

Thwack! Exquisite pain roared at the small of his back.

She wants to flog me until I look like a victim of the Spanish Inquisition?

He could get into that. Charlotte cradled her massive breast in one hand and swung the flogger with the other. He watched her hips gyrate as her butterfly worked on her clit and pussy lips, bringing forth a rash of goose bumps and nipples as dark as erasers.

She's close to coming, and she's getting off on beating the holy hell out of me.

This was what he wanted, his closest friends and exciting lovers in his home, every night. Although it would be hard to pin down Charlotte and Lina, since catching those two was like capturing a whirlwind, he knew they would become fixtures in his home.

He turned onto his knees as Grant pushed him into a new position. Lina pulled away from his cock, much to his dismay, but he quickly forgot his disappointment as Grant poured some lube onto his index finger and gently inserted it in his ass. He pressed and prodded until Sam loosened and relaxed. Then Grant slathered on some lube and entered him gently from behind.

Lina slipped a condom onto Luke, who lay on the rug next to him. She straddled his dancer's body to ride him cowgirl style, and then she slid him inside her. She fingered her clit as she rocked back and forth, turning to Sam and flashing him her most alluring smile.

Sam closed his eyes. *Yes, this is what I want, more pain and pleasure combined, good friends, and hot sex.*

Thwack! The sting on his back sent his heart jumping. The ghost of pain seared his back. He felt welts growing on his skin. Charlotte branded him with that flogger.

"Do you like this, Sam?"

"Yes, I love it."

"Do you deserve more?'

"I hope so. I—"

Thwack!

"Does Grant feel good inside you?"

"Yes."

"Do you like getting fucked up the ass?" Her breathy voice heightened and became so aroused he barely heard her.

"I love it."

"Can you feel his cock jamming you inside? Does it feel so damned good?" She pushed the butterfly hard against her clit. Gasping for breath, she writhed in front of him on the verge of climax.

Damn she looks so sexy right before she bursts. "Yes . . . Oh!"

"Do you like being fucked up your dirty hole?" She ran her fingers through her long coffee-colored hair, head raised, bedroom eyes at half-mast, mouth open in a rictus of ecstasy.

"Yes." *Now I'm out of breath.*

"I want you to suck me off, luv."

"Then get over here."

She ground the butterfly into her pussy lips so hard he feared she'd hurt herself. Instead, her body coiled as if it were a spring, and she tore the butterfly down until it buzzed at her knees.

"Aaaaaaahhhh! I'm coming! Quick, eat me."

Charlotte lay on her back on the floor, spread her legs, and wiggled until her pussy pressed against Sam's face. She tasted of musk that smeared over his cheeks as he shoved his tongue hard against her clit, rubbing in tight little circles as she writhed around him. He slid two fingers in her snatch, then three, then four. She was so hot and wet she nearly took in his entire fist. He flicked her clit with his tongue and thumb at once, giving her a double dose of erotic bliss.

Grant slammed his cock so hard in his ass Sam nearly

doubled over on the rug, but he held fast. His own erection grew harder and harder. His skin thickened, and his cock grew broad and hard as a pipe. Once Grant reached his prostate, that was all it took. With a cry, Grant shot his load with Sam, pulling out to spurt his cum onto the welts on Sam's back. Jizz warmed Sam's skin from his lower back to his shoulder blades.

Grant always could carry the distance.

Charlotte relaxed in Sam's embrace, her gyrations easing until she pulled away and curled into a fetal position on the rug next to him. Grant lay on the couch. Lena and Luke had already finished and were watching them, delighted expressions on their amused faces.

"I'd love to make you three a habit," Charlotte said. "Especially now that I know you're beasts in every sense of the word."

Sam sighed with relief. Charlotte and Lina took to them after all, despite a rocky start. His instincts were correct. He, Grant, and Luke had the two women in their corner. Five friends who could never be torn apart enjoyed each other for the next hour before Luke, Lina, and Charlotte returned home.

Sam and Grant had finished cleaning up when frantic knocking sounded at the door. Wondering why Charlotte and Lina had returned in such a harried fashion, Sam raced to the door. Grant looked out the side window.

Willow stood outside, eyes wide and terrified.

"I can't deal with this." Willow ran past Grant after he opened the door. She collapsed on the couch in a folded-up bundle of quaking nerves. She had partially shifted and wasn't taking the change well. "Please, make it stop."

Grant raced across the room and sat next to her. He took her in his arms, and she cried with great whooping gasps of air. "Sweetie, there's nothing you can do except get through it. You're not alone." Her claws dug into his bare chest, drawing a thin line of blood. He pulled her hand away. "Easy there, girl. You're hurting me."

"I'm sorry. I can't help it. I think I scratched up your door, too."

Sam sat on her opposite side. "Don't worry about that. We've done enough damage to that door on our own. When did you start shifting?"

"About three hours ago. I drank as much of the monkshood rye as I could, but I threw it all up. I'm not used to hard liquor. I don't drink much."

"Yeah, that stuff is pretty strong, especially for someone as small as you," He smiled and squeezed her shoulder. "We're big, strapping, buff stage crew dudes. You're just a wisp of a thing."

"I didn't know what else to do so I ran into the woods. I got lost but I found the main road and followed it until I got here," she said.

"How'd you know where we live?" Grant asked.

"Luke told me during a rehearsal. I know this area. I like to go for walks around the lake behind your house to clear my head."

"We'll show you how to get to the quarry. That's the safest place. No one goes out that far, since the hiking and bike paths don't pass near it and hunting is forbidden around it." Sam said. "You sound a little calmer. Would you like something to drink? Cola? Hot tea?"

"Hot tea sounds good."

"How about some Chinese black tea? It's very tasty." Sam said. He walked to the kitchen.

"Restaurant quality." Grant boasted.

"That sounds good." Willow sat up and slouched on the couch.

One look at her, and Grant knew they were in for a long night. She looked like a frightened child. Her face was as pale and round as the full moon. Shadows lurked below her sunken grey eyes. Her auburn hair had thickened and fell in an unkempt pile to her shoulders. Her jeans were torn, and her t-shirt had ripped down the back. She stuck her pinkie finger in her mouth and gnawed at the claw that grew there. Grant took her hand in both of his and placed it in her lap. He recalled her saying she chewed her nails when she was nervous, which was all the time. It was odd that even nail biters grew long, sharp claws when they shifted.

Willow sighed, a dejected sound. Shoulders slumped, the poor girl looked defeated. Grant feared for her. This was only her second month shifting. He and Sam needed to mentor her and guide her, otherwise she would not survive to the end of the season.

"Let's take all this a little at a time," Grant said. "You're looking at it as one big problem, which is why you're overwhelmed. Think only about tonight. You made it here. That's a good start."

"I don't know what to do. I don't feel good." She grasped her stomach.

"Part of that is the shifting," Grant said. "The other could be you getting sick from the monkshood rye drink."

Sam returned to the couch and sat to her side opposite Grant. "Water's on. It'll be tea in ten. How about I put some monkshood in tea form for you, since you don't drink alcohol? That will ease some of your symptoms."

"Okay, I'll try it." Willow said. "Anything to stop feeling like I'm going out of my mind."

"I have fresh peppermint. That will kill some of the graveyard dirt taste. I suspected you were a lightweight, but I didn't know for sure. Grant and I will stick to monkshood rye, but it's monkshood black tea with peppermint for you. I'll mix it."

"You have an advantage over us, actually," Grant told her.

"How?" Willow asked.

Grant smiled. "Tea is a hell of a lot less expensive than rye."

She smiled her first smile of the night. It didn't make her look any less frazzled, but it was a vast improvement over abject depression.

"The first thing we have to do is get you out of those torn clothes." Grant said. He stood and walked to his bedroom. In moments he returned with a bundle of clothing in his arms. "Here's a fresh t-shirt and drawstring sweatpants for you. Sorry I can't give you underwear." He grinned. "I don't swing that way."

She laughed and sounded more relaxed. *Good, get her laughing to ease her tension.*

"My panties are fine. They're stretchy. I don't wear a bra. Not enough to put into one."

"You look fine," Sam said. "Why don't you take the clothes into the bathroom and change? By the time you come back out, it'll almost be teatime."

She retreated with the clothing to their bathroom. Grant followed Sam into the kitchen.

"So much for getting any sleep tonight," Sam said. "I don't think we'd get much anyway since I feel an overwhelming urge to shift. Full moon at its peak, you know."

"Why don't we invite her to run along with us? We can avoid the crowded areas. Stick to the quiet side of the lake and the quarry."

"Sounds like a plan. We can burn off the urge and get back home a little before dawn. Then sleep in. Good thing we don't have to work until late afternoon."

The tea kettle whistled, and Sam grabbed it. He poured steaming water into an oversized mug with a tea bag, a tea ball full of monkshood, and four peppermint stalks. Willow appeared in the living room looking waifish in Grant's clothing. His heart warmed toward her, seeing her looking like a disheveled date the day after the party ended. He didn't think of her as a date, though. She was the little sister he never had. As she tugged at the waistband of his sweatpants that were too big for her, she gave him a wry smile.

"How can I ever thank you both?" she asked.

"It's not necessary," Grant said. "Your tea is almost ready. Once you drink it, you'll feel better. Then we can go for a run."

"A run?"

"Yes. The three of us can shift and run in the woods at this hour because it's quiet out. At least it will be where we're going."

"Where are we going?"

"To the lake and quarry and the woods around them. Only one side, though—the side away from the bike and hiking paths. It's very peaceful there. You'll see. It's a clear night, too. We can star gaze. I understand there's a meteor shower tonight."

"That sounds like fun," Willow said. "I wish I didn't have to shift, though. I'd enjoy it more."

"Don't be so sure," Grant said. "Your senses will be enhanced. You'll see the sky much better in wolf form than in human form. It'll be stunning."

"Your tea's ready." Sam removed the herbs and handed her the mug. "How's it taste?"

She sipped gingerly, avoiding the heat. "Not bad. The peppermint helps. It still has that nice bouquet of freshly dug crime scene, though."

"With a high metallic note. We know." Sam said. "It'll grow on you."

"Like fungus." Grant said.

She laughed again, second time that night. Grant was thrilled they'd made progress. He was determined to get her to relax. He'd never had a younger sibling, and he had always wanted a little sister to call his own. He had to be careful, though. Willow was so tiny and delicate. He was tempted to treat her like a china doll, but he knew that would only upset her. He had a strong suspicion plenty of people had underestimated her, thinking she was weak because of the way she was built. If her dancing was any indication of her strength, she had nothing to worry about.

"Drink up, then let's head out," Sam said. "You might want to head to the local thrift store and stock up on very loose clothing. We rely on it this time of month. As you've already found out, clothing that fits tears when we shift. Grant and I have taken to wife-beaters, oversized t's, stretchy shorts, and sweatpants."

"Where's the thrift store?" Willow asked. "I love thrift stores."

"A girl after my own heart." Grant said, happy he'd found something else in common with her. He loved shopping in thrift stores. It was like treasure hunting. He never knew what he'd find. Once he found an electric juicer for $3.00 that was brand new. In a regular store, it would have cost $30.00. "I'll take you the next time we have free time during the day. It's a great place. All the rich locals take their clothes and stuff there. You know the type. They wouldn't be caught dead wearing the same thing twice."

"I'm sold." Willow said as she finished her tea. She placed the mug on the kitchen counter. "What do we do now?"

"We roam," Sam said.

Grant was right—the sky was stunning. Willow raced along behind Sam and Grant as they made their way through thick bramble. Since she had partially shifted, her skin had thickened, so the thorns didn't scratch her. She felt no pain. To be out and about in the dead of night with her two newest friends actually felt free. Hell, Grant and Sam were her only friends, not including Luke whom she didn't know as well. She never was one for getting overly attached to people. She'd been burned far too often. Trust was a big issue for her, as in she didn't have any. When was the last time she'd relied on anyone for anything, aside from the man who changed her? Look how that turned out.

They made their way through the woods until they reached the clearing near the quarry. Oaks and maples towered overhead. A few scattered pine trees had dropped pinecones and needles on the earth. Willow grabbed a few blackberries from a bush to her left and popped them into her mouth. Their tart taste exploded on her tongue, a more intense flavor than she expected. It was like eating sunlight. That was what Grant and Sam meant by enhanced senses. Her taste buds were in overdrive. Crickets and nightpeepers sang in the dark. A light breeze blew through the treetops.

From the clearing, stars twinkled in the night sky. The Milky Way carved a bright band through the heavens. Sam and Grant were right. The stars shone with more intensity in her shifted form. A meteor streaked across the sky. She swore she heard the woosh as it sailed by.

The full moon hung high in the sky, mocking her.

I'll beat you. I have friends in my corner now. You can't scare me.

"I'm hot," Willow said.

"That's why we're at the quarry," Sam said. "Want a dip in the nice, cool water?"

"I'd love it. Anything to get this sweat off me."

"Last one in's a rotten egg," Grant said in a stage whisper. It was wise not to shout when they needed to remain hidden. He ran to the quarry and jumped in, followed by Sam. Willow brought up the rear as usual, being a bit slow on the uptake.

The water cooled her hot body. She felt energy she hadn't felt in months. Being with two new friends helped. As she doggy paddled her way to them, she watched the sky. Two meteors zipped by.

"Hey, did you see that?" she asked.

"No, what?" Grant said.

"Meteors."

"Let's head for the rocks by the outcropping," Sam said. "We can watch without any danger of us being seen."

Willow followed, then made herself comfortable lying on a boulder half in and half out of the water.

This is the life. I could get used to this in a hurry. If shifting always feels so good I won't mind it so much. "Is it always like this for you two?" she asked.

"Like what?" Grant asked.

"Peaceful."

"Far from it," Sam said. "I don't know what I'd do if I didn't have Grant. He's my anchor."

"Same for me," Grant said. "Sam's my soul mate."

"But you take lovers," Willow said.

"We're negotiable," Grant said with a smile.

"If you're wondering, we don't think of you as a lover. You're our pet," Sam said.

She laughed. "I'm a helpless kitten in need of care."

"That's not too far off the mark," Grant said. "We'd be happy to mentor you. You're doing fine right now. Just know it won't always be so easy. That's why we're here. We'll protect you."

"Thank you. I normally don't let anyone get so close, but I trust you two."

Grant wrapped a big arm around her, and she leaned her head against his shoulder. The three of them lay back and watched the heavens. A meteor flashed across the sky.

"Oh, another one," Sam said. "Big one, too."

"I saw it," Willow said. "There's another one."

"And a third," Grant said. "I heard this was supposed to be the best shower in two decades."

"It's delivering," Sam said.

They spent the next hour enjoying the shower from the safety and seclusion of their rocky outcropping. No one saw them. Hunters did not whoop and holler with a blood thirst for wolves. Although Willow relished relaxing with Grant and Sam, her rumbling stomach had ideas of its own.

"I'm hungry," she said. "It's very uncomfortable. I feel an overpowering urge to attack something."

"It's the need for raw meat. I know just the place to hunt," Grant said. "Let's dry off and get back into our clothes. I could use a late-night dinner myself."

Soon they raced through the woods again, with Willow bringing up the rear. They reached a thicket not far from the quarry when Grant signaled them to stop. "I hear something in the underbrush," he whispered.

"Are we in trouble?" Willow asked.

"No. It's dinner."

"Smells like turkey. I could go for an early Thanksgiving," Sam said.

"Stick to the wildlife when you hunt, Willow," Grant said. "I know you've eaten livestock. That gets you on human radar. Don't eat anything that costs humans money. No livestock. No pets. No matter how tempting."

"Got it. That was a huge mistake on my part. I knew it after I did it."

"It's all right. You got away with it that time. Just don't do it again. Okay, let's nail this bird."

"Watch me. I'm a master," Sam said.

"Says you. I'll get that bird on the first try," Grant said.

"Fifty bucks says you don't."

"You're on."

Grant crouched on all fours, hackles up, nostrils flared.

There was nothing more glorious than being on the hunt when he wasn't disturbed by hunters or other interlopers. His improved vision from shifting helped him spy the unsuspecting turkey that somehow had gotten away from its rafter. He'd seen this rafter before. It amounted to about twelve wild turkeys. Grant knew if he missed this one the others couldn't be far away, but he wanted to impress Willow so much — and pry that fifty bucks out of Sam's smug hands — that he wanted to catch this one on the first try.

Besides, they'd eat well tonight if he caught it. Sure beat another diet of 'possum or raccoon. He and Sam didn't make a habit of going for the turkeys, since there were so few. One during the summer and one for November's full moon. That gave the rafters time to replenish in the spring. Every turkey they snared was replaced by a brand new one.

Grant skulked through the brush, belly to the wet, cold earth. The bird was only a couple of yards ahead of him. When it turned its back to him, he raced toward it and pounced. The bird squawked and flew, but Grant leaped in the air, catching it in his claws and teeth. It was one of his better leaps. He knew how impressive he looked when he soared into the air in full wolfen form.

Here he was, trying to impress a woman he wasn't trying to bed.

The bird struggled for only a second before Grant broke its neck. Once it was on the ground, Sam and Willow rushed over. Grant and Sam pawed at the turkey to remove its feathers. Willow watched, her head cocked to one side.

"It's barbaric," she said.

"We gotta eat. It's actually quick and painless," Grant said. "We don't want the animals to suffer."

"Help us remove the feathers. The only thing worse than feathers between your teeth is hair," Sam said.

"I'm not touching that one," Grant said with a laugh.

"You two get your minds out of the gutter." Willow said as she clawed away clumps of feathers and down.

Once the bird was ready, they ate with gusto. Grant would have preferred the turkey roasted with green bean casserole and candied sweet potatoes, but when in Lycan form he needed raw, bloody meat. This bird fit the bill. He relaxed as he ate, keeping an ear out for trespassers. He heard nothing but the wind in the trees and the crickets in the grass. The plaintive wail of a screech owl cried in the distance.

Here he was with his lover and adopted sister, enjoying a hearty meal under a clear, starry sky. This was the good life. He wanted this evening to last forever, but sadly the moon was approaching the horizon, meaning dawn was coming.

As the pink sheen of the rising sun glowed in the sky, Sam, Grant, and Willow made their way back to Grant and Sam's home by the lake. They raced past trees and the quarry to swim their way through the lake where it stopped at the forest behind their home. They climbed a hill until they reached the backyard. By the time they made it into their home, it was five-forty. Willow slipped into the oversized shirt Grant had given her, and Sam escorted her to the guest bedroom. By six all three were asleep, dreaming of running together through a beautiful and safe forest.

CHAPTER SIXTEEN

R ising Action: (n) A related series of incidents in a literary
plot that build toward the climax.
Rising Action: (n) Getting an erection.

Sam was relieved when the last night of the full moon arrived.
It would all be over in twenty-four hours. Although he enjoyed his time with Willow and Grant, there was no chance
he'd ever get used to the monthly shifting, no matter how
hard he tried, even after years of constant change. If he didn't
like it, how would Willow cope?

By noon that afternoon, he and Grant stood in the catwalks,
adjusting shutters on a few lamps.

"Dress rehearsal shouldn't be too bad," Grant said. "The
worst is over. All we have to do is position the lamps, and
we're set."

"Easier said than done, but I agree. Getting the stage
prepped was time-consuming enough. I expect us to be finished by ten tonight."

"You got the rye with you?"

Sam patted the water bottle on his hip. "You bet I do.
There's a jug of it in my car if you need more."

"I think I'll be fine, but it's good to have it on hand. Ah,
here's the director. Let's get ready. I'll take stage left, and you
take stage right."

"It's a deal."

He walked into the shadows stage left and peered onto the

stage below. Dancers stretched and flexed, each one in his or her own world. He loved to watch the dancers as they warmed up. Such grace was not rare in the theater, but it was uncommon in the rest of the world. They made it look so easy. If only he could lift his legs like that so that his knees touched his ears. Such movement would surely make his love life much more interesting.

The director started at stage right, giving Sam more time to observe. He admired Grant's physique as he adjusted shutters on an especially stubborn lamp. While he didn't have the grace Luke had, his movements revealed the power and strength he carried so effortlessly. Grant could carry heavier equipment than Sam, and Sam envied that ability. They didn't compete with each other — a rarity in the theater — but that didn't stop Sam from doing his best to keep up with his lover. Now the two of them were working together to help a kindred spirit. They so seldom met others like them that they had grown used to being alone.

Not anymore.

Willow sat on the stage, arching her back as she gracefully slid into a split. Watching her made Sam's thighs ache. He could never sit like that, even if he wanted to. What must it have been like for her for the past two months, having been so isolated? Aside from sheer terror, her confusion must have overwhelmed her. He remembered his first few times shifting. He no longer controlled his body, and that lack of control humiliated and scared him. If there was anything he, and especially Grant, craved above all, it was control over their bodies, their careers, their very lives. However, he knew in life there was no real control over anything. Outside factors always got in the way.

Then there was the shame he felt over his changing body. It was worse than when he was a teenager with gangling, growing limbs in search of adequate motor control. Each shifting left him feeling vulnerable and exposed, especially when he couldn't stop it once it was in full swing. Had Willow hidden in the desert in around Vegas when her Lycan side took over? She must have. What else could she possibly have done? All alone in a desert populated by scorpions, rattle-snakes, and prickly cactus could not have been pleasant.

At least now, she didn't have to be alone. If she ended up alone, it would be by her choice. He didn't think she wanted solitude, though, especially after he and Luke spent time with her at the Black Horse. She seemed like such an awkward lit-tle thing, his adopted baby sister. Despite her ability to shift, she was repulsed at her abilities and wouldn't take advantage of her curse.

It was not good for her to be alone, since she was so green. Tonight, he knew he had to grab her before the moon rose. If she shifted alone, he feared she'd panic and go into melt-down. Sam, Grant, and Luke were there to help her and keep her company, which pleased Sam no end. Protective of the young dancer, he felt a kinship with her he didn't often feel with the cast and crew of the shows he lit.

Sam and Grant finished adjusting the lamps and shutters in the catwalks within an hour, a quick turnaround that sur-prised them both. Normally, dress rehearsals took hours to resolve. Not this one. Sam was thrilled to work with such an efficient director. The woman had lighting experience. She knew exactly what she wanted, and Sam was happy to give it to her. Next came adjusting the lamps hanging on the trees in the wings, so he and Grant returned to the stage.

When Sam set foot in the stage left wing, he saw Willow standing not far from him. She was sipping a hot drink, stand-ing behind a curtain, minding her own business as she usually did. "Hey, kid, how you holding up?" he asked.

"Not too bad. I'll need a shower after rehearsal. I'm sweat-ing up a storm."

"Any hint you'll shift soon?"

"I don't feel it coming, but I'm sure I will before the night is over."

"Did you make some of the monkshood drink?"

"Yes. It does help." She held up her cup. "I'm drinking it now. It's more tolerable hot, and I like it as tea much better than with rye. The urge to shift isn't strong right now. I can relax and get my work done." She grimaced. "That stuff tastes like low tide and dead fish, though. How do you stomach it?"

He laughed. "I don't. I tolerate it since I need it so much. Don't worry. After tonight, you won't need it for another month."

"Great. Twenty-eight more days and I turn into The Beast of Exmoor again. It never ends, does it?"

"No, I'm sorry, it doesn't. I don't know how to break the curse. Neither does Grant."

"You asked him to turn you? Why?"

"Because I love him."

She smiled. "That's very sweet. Maybe I'll be so lucky someday."

"Maybe. You never know." The director waved everyone back on stage. "You want to meet at the Black Horse after rehearsal? We should stick together on nights like this."

"I need to get home and shower first. I can join you about eleven-thirty. How's that sound?"

"It's a plan. See you after rehearsal."

Without warning, she walked to Sam and wrapped her arms around him. His heart lurched, feeling an overwhelming urge to hug her so tightly she complained she couldn't breathe. With a start, he realized he loved his little sister. He wanted to care for her and look after her for the rest of their lives.

"You, Grant, and Luke have been so good to me," she said with tears in her voice. "I haven't felt this close to anyone else in such a long time. Just know I appreciate all you're doing for me."

Before he could respond, she raced for center stage. Warmth filled his body—the warmth of friendship and caring. It was only a fleeting impression, but he wondered if he could talk Willow into staying in Portland once the tour was finished. He hadn't talked to Grant yet about staying put, but the more he thought about it, the more he liked the idea. The trendy nature of Portland, the progressive politics, the generally positive GLBT atmosphere, and the impressive mountains drew him in. Willow would probably benefit from living in the area. She needed the companionship, and she'd miss it if she left with the road show. He decided to talk to her later that night to see what she thought of his idea.

When Sam and Grant walked into the Black Horse Pub at eleven, the smell of beer and deep-fried onion rings slammed into Sam like a wall. The roughnecks playing darts and pool in the back made a ruckus. Sam wondered what had agitated them.

Luke waved from a group of tables next to the windows. Sam and Grant weaved their way through the crowd and took two seats next to Luke and across from Charlotte and Lina. Sam worried that there was no sign of Willow. A group of very drunken men gathered near the front door, caterwauling with so much energy Sam feared they'd break out in a fight. Their dogs moved in impatient circles around them, baying as if they couldn't wait to get out the door.

Sam feared he knew what was up, but he had to ask. "What's going on? What's got everyone so worked up?"

"There was another wolf sighting," Lina said. "Those guys are going to try to kill it."

"As much as they've had to drink tonight, they're more likely to kill each other," Luke said.

Sam went cold inside and glanced at Grant who gave him the same knowing look. The wolf had to be Willow. How could he possibly keep these thugs from killing her without getting shot in the process?

"Are you thinking what I'm thinking?" Grant asked.

"Yes," Sam said. "We can't sit here and let them assassinate her. We have to do something."

"I told her to meet us here after rehearsal. She was going home first to shower. I don't know where she is, but she shouldn't be too hard to track. Plus, we're not nearly as wasted as they are. Do you have the rye with you?"

"It's on my belt. I have enough to last the rest of the night."

"Me, too. Let's get going so we get ahead of that lynch mob."

"You guys just got here. You're leaving already?" Charlotte asked as they stood and moved away from the table.

"We forgot something. We'll be back as soon as we can," Sam said.

"I'll save these two seats for you," Luke said. "Don't be long." He nodded at them, his signal that he knew what they were planning.

"I hope we won't be," Grant said.

Sam and Grant shoved their way past the drunks and their dogs. The sour mash smell of booze made Sam's head woozy. While the drunks argued over how to proceed, Sam and Grant made their way for the woods. If they partially shifted, they could follow her scent and not tear through their clothes as they grew.

They shifted with ease and raced for the deepest part of the woods, following Willow's scent. The scent of a werewolf was stronger and more pungent than that of a human. While dogs could detect it, werewolves could follow it with much more ease. Hopefully, Willow had made it to the lake and hidden in the cool water, which would mask her scent from the dogs but not from Grant and Sam.

Instead, as they followed her scent, Sam was horrified to discover she had taken the hiking paths away from the lake and headed for Mountain Road. Not good. Too many tourists and drunken hunters out that way. Why hadn't she listened to him? He'd told her to avoid public areas. The hiking paths near Mountain Road were very public. She'd be seen for sure, especially with all that rich auburn fur and her shining yellow eyes.

She might have panicked and ran into the wrong direction by accident, but what if she did it on purpose? What if she wanted to put herself in harm's way? Why would she do that? Sam didn't want to think of the reasons that flashed by his mind. Best to shake off the alarm and find her.

Sam feared in tracking down Willow, he and Grant could expose themselves to the hunters and end up getting shot themselves. What a horrid predicament they found himself in.

Whooping and hollering echoed nearby. Gunshots rang in the air. The hunters were not far away. Sam feared for Willow's life as well as his own and Grant's.

"We have to find her now," Sam said. "If we don't, all three of us could get killed."

"Those yahoos are liable to shoot anything that crosses their paths," Grant said. "Can you catch her scent?"

Sam sniffed the air and detected a faint musky smell beneath citrus-scented soap. His sense of smell was so sensitive he could practically determine which brand of shampoo she used. "Yes, but barely. She's bathed, and I wish she hadn't. She'd be easier to locate if she hadn't cleaned herself."

"She must be a nervous wreck by now, especially since she likely has no idea how to find us. She can't go to the pub in her condition. Maybe she can smell us much easier than we can smell her. Hopefully her nose will lead her straight to us."

"Assuming the dogs don't find us first."

"Or her."

Sam and Grant had not yet showered, so they wore their sweat like a badge. Sam followed what little of Willow's scent he could detect and raced with Grant toward the same copse of bushes by Mountain Road where they'd first met her. As he had expected, she was cowering in the bushes, shivering with fright by the time they found her.

"Willow!" Grant said in a stage whisper so he wouldn't be overheard by the hunters. "Follow us to the lake. It's not safe here."

"I can't do this," she wailed.

"Not so loud. They'll find you," Sam said.

"I can't stop shaking. All I want to do is eat, and I need meat. Raw, bloody meat. I hate the taste. It's nauseating. I hate myself. I don't want to live like this."

"I know it's hard—"

"It's worse than that. I was wrong. I don't want this. I want it to end. Now."

"Please trust us." Sam begged. "Don't do anything rash. Just follow us to the lake. We can help you through this."

"No one can."

"It won't be easy, but we're here for you. There are only a few more hours of night, then it's over."

"For twenty-eight days. Then it starts all over again. I can't take it."

"Yes, you can," Grant called, a little too loudly. Sam hushed him. "Please, follow us now. The hunters are closing in, and they'll kill all of us if we don't haul ass right now."

Gunshots roared, sounding closer than they'd been only moments before. Dogs bayed, closing in on their scents. Sam took a path in the direction of the quarry, but in her panic, Willow ran in the opposite direction along a path leading to the main road.

"No! Not that way!" Sam called.

He and Grant rushed through the bramble, staying as low as possible so the drunken crowd would not see them, but Willow far outpaced them.

Smaller and more limber, she ran faster. Following her scent, they sped along the path until her scent took them on an unexpected turn toward the quarry. Maybe she had listened to Sam after all and corrected her path. Hope welled in Sam's bosom. Maybe, just maybe, the three of them could reach the quarry and hide in the cool water until the riled-up crowd settled down and left. The closer he and Grant raced approached the quarry, the calmer he felt. Yes, they would make it.

Then he heard the gunshot and a cry. A human female cry. *No! No! Not her! Please, let her live.*

They crouched behind a group of boulders, hidden from the marauders. Once his breath eased and his heart ceased pounding, Sam reverted to his human form. Grant stooped next to him, shaking his head as his Lycan form retreated into his human one. They remained motionless and silent. Sam shivered with fright, fearing the worst and knowing there was nothing he could do about it. He had never felt so helpless. Sam turned to stare at Grant, looking for any cue for an appropriate time to rise and greet the hunters. Grant nodded, and they stood and emerged from behind the rocks. They blended in with the hunting party in their loose clothing. As they weaved their way through the crowd, Sam spotted a small, pale arm and a thatch of thick, red hair.

Willow lay face-down, milky-white skin glowing pale in the moonlight. Mud caked to her skin, which was covered with scratches. An angry hole gaped in the center of her back. Sam went cold inside, feeling the loss of a new friend but unable to express his grief.

"Who is she, and what was she doing out here?" one of the hunters asked.

The image shows the word "Black" written in italic serif font.

"I saw a wolf. I shot at a wolf," another said with confusion and guilt in his voice.

Voices faded into noise. Sam and Grant approached Willow, and Grant removed his jacket. One of the hunters took a few steps toward Willow, and Grant stood in his path.

"Get away from her," he said in a raspy voice.

The hunter did not argue with him. Grant knelt on one knee and placed his jacket over her.

"She must have been skinny-dipping and didn't hear any of you." He made up any excuse to prevent the hunters from questioning her presence too much.

"Do you know her?" one of the crowd asked, his voice quiet with distress.

"She's in the dance troupe we work with."

"We need to get her back to town," Sam said. "We can't just leave her here."

"Call the police," Grant said. "We'll wait here with her until they arrive."

By the time Sam and Grant returned home, Sam wanted to fall in bed and sleep for the next hundred years. He blamed himself. What could he have done to prevent Willow's death? True, she'd panicked and ran in the wrong direction, but he could have stepped in sooner and taken control of the situation. He hadn't, and now the only other werewolf he'd met aside of Grant was dead. It was his fault.

Would things really have been much different for Willow if Sam had grown closer to her? What happened was tragic. She was terribly green and naïve, and she wanted to die. Her death wish was something he could neither control nor overcome. Had he really had any control over Willow's life? He smiled, realizing the arrogance of his intentions. Of course not.

She'd made her own destiny, and events out of her control made her decision for her. He realized he didn't know her as well as he thought he had. Maybe she'd intended to go out in a blaze of gunfire after all. She made it clear she couldn't bear shifting month after month for many years and decades and possibly centuries down the road. Sam would never know. Questions and thoughts of what could have been would torment him for the rest of his life if he let them.

Let go. That's all I can do. I have Grant and now Luke. Lina, and Charlotte. Cherish the friends I do have. Make the most of a bad situation.

CHAPTER SEVENTEEN

Pick-up: (n) When attached to an acoustic musical instrument, a pick-up converts sound vibrations into an electrical signal.
Pick-up: (v) To meet someone in a bar, party, rave, or similar place, then talk that person into leaving to have sex.

The five friends sat in a booth in the Black Horse Pub, drinking their sorrows away. Grant stared out the window, numb. Friday night was normally a fun party night, but death had cast a pall over him. Light rain fell. The sound carried through the window as if trying to sooth him but didn't succeed.

"Production can't be postponed, since the show is in three weeks, but the director has given everyone the weekend off," Luke said. "I'm glad. I don't think I can function well at all at the moment."

"We were just getting to know her," Sam said. "It's not fair. She had friends who could have stood by her side."

"She was too far gone to see that," Grant said. "I wish she'd trusted us more."

"I didn't know her at all, but I watched her dance. She was very graceful," Charlotte said. "Made it look effortless."

"I didn't know her, either," Lina said. "You guys have more exposure to dancers and actors than we do. Most of the painting work is done without performers nearby."

"She was a rising star," Luke said. "She could have gone places. Her shyness got in her way. She was opening up, though. I was looking forward to getting to know her better." He took a deep swallow of pilsner and sighed. "This is making me feel really miserable. I feel so guilty, like I should have done something but didn't."

Regret slammed into Grant like a wall. Really, what could any of them have done? Not much. Her life, so full of promise, snuffed out far too short. She didn't smile often, so when she did, he'd taken pleasure in it. Her smile lit up her face for a second, then disappeared so quickly it was as if she never beamed at all. Darkness followed her so closely light couldn't get in.

With a start, he saw much of himself in Willow's perpetual sadness. For decades following his own change, he had drifted along in his life, barely living, not knowing what lay ahead for him, dreading the full moon, and foolishly believing he could go back to the way things were. He had come very close to ending his own life on numerous occasions.

Then he'd met Sam, who had saved his life.

Why couldn't Willow allow her new friends to calm her, to be her buffer from the reality of a cruel and uncaring world?

He'd never know.

As if reading his mind, Sam leaned into Grant. "Just when she was starting to warm up to us, this crap happens." Sam said.

"Could we really have done anything else to help her?" Lina asked. "Are you sure we aren't beating ourselves up too much?"

"I doubt we could have done much more," Grant said. "We got to know her too late." He sipped his scotch, his drink of choice when he was upset. He'd already gone through a third of the bottle. Anything to numb the pain. "She felt like the little sister I never had. I wanted to protect her, and I failed."

"Stop talking like that," Luke said. "We're not doing ourselves any good by thinking that way. I don't think Willow would like it, either. She could be very morose, but I saw lightness in her she let out only around us."

"I saw it, too," Charlotte said. "She always seemed to be happy and relaxed around you guys, even if it was only for a few days. The change was very noticeable. Her face lit up whenever you came around. I want to remember her that way." She smiled and placed one hand on Grant's shoulder. "She was loved, and she knew it. You were alike in very important ways."

"You're right. We could relate to her in ways no one else in the company could," Grant said. "Hell, probably like no one else in town. I mean, seriously, how many more werewolves are we likely to run into around here?" He laughed, and pent-up tension released so quickly it took him by surprise. He couldn't stop laughing.

The mood spread. Luke snickered into his ale. "I bet she'd never have been able to eat venison around us again with a straight face."

"And you forced her to eat it," Sam said with a laugh. "Not one of your relatives? That was brilliant."

"I learned from her to value my friendships. I won't take anyone for granted anymore." Grant turned to Sam and hugged him. "She made me realize how lucky I am to have you, lover. You're my soul mate, and we have the best friends anyone could ever have." Overwhelmed with love, he fought the quiver in his voice and continued. "I usually form intense but superficial relationships with people in the show, and the closeness ends the moment the last curtain goes down and we go our separate ways. Not anymore." Happiness overflowed inside him, making his heart race. "Let's never lose touch, no matter where we end up."

"That brings me to something I've wanted to talk about for some time now," Sam turned to Grant. "What do you say we stay here year-round and stop following the tours? I mean for a few years?"

"I was thinking that very thing myself," Grant said. "I wouldn't mind putting down roots here. Portland is gorgeous and very friendly. I've outgrown my wanderlust. Besides, we have good friends." He nodded at Luke, "Another shifter who can identify with us, and lots of hot sex."

"Aren't you guys in a group?" Luke asked. "I mean most of your kind . . ."

"They're called packs, and no, we've never been in a pack," Sam said. "We've always been strictly loners. Following the tours, we've never stuck to one place long enough to be in a pack. Besides, the packs I've seen were full of pretentious jerkoffs who weren't careful when they shifted, and they could have gotten *us* killed. No thanks. I haven't needed anyone but Grant."

"We'd like to add you three to our little private club," Grant turned to Charlotte and Lina. "I know you were thinking about relocating, and if you chose here, there's an added benefit for you two. Being shifters, we can go all night—much longer than a human male."

"I'm sold." Charlotte's grin revealed her lust beneath those two simple words.

"Count me in," Lina said as she wrapped her arms around Charlotte's waist.

Grant smiled. *They look as good together as Sam, Luke, and I. All five of us belong together. Friends, lovers, protectors.*

"Count me in, too," Luke said. "I'm another loner. Don't know any other deer shifters in this area, and I seriously doubt there are any. And . . . I have a surprise."

"What?" Sam asked, his hand going to Grant's thigh.

Grant reached down and squeezed his hand. Overwhelmed with emotion, he took a swallow of his scotch to keep the tears at bay.

"I've had an offer from a local company to be their lead dancer and choreographer. I'd love to choreograph some ballet. I wasn't sure whether or not to take the job. Now I've made my decision. I'm staying here. I begin after this tour ends."

Joy rose in Grant's heart. *Two fantastic men who tend to my every need. Two women who can't be pinned down yet make room in their lives for me. Why not settle down here?*

"In that case, I have a great way for us to celebrate," Charlotte called for a waiter.

When the bottle of champagne arrived with a tray with five glasses, she poured, handing a glass to each of them. Grant held his glass high and stole a glance at Sam, who smiled with contentment.

"Let's have a toast," she said. "To Willow, who brought us all together, and to our new life not wandering all over the earth the way we used to. Let's get this party started. I know you guys can go all night."

And they did.

The End

Excerpt

"Hey, Rasta-man!" Spud yelled. "When you gonna cut your hair?"

"When you get manners, Murphy," Alex replied, sitting at his usual table, eyeing the locals and the two strangers across the room huddled in the corner booth. Out-of-towners. He didn't like their look. And the way they glanced at him, the feeling was mutual.

Spud sauntered over and pulled out a chair, turned it about and straddled it, his arms resting on the back. "Seen any little green men lately?"

"Nope." Alex sighed. Everyone knew that his hobby was sitting out on his roof at night with his telescope. And given that he subscribed to Science Fiction Monthly magazine, ordered in especially by the local newsagent — Spud's brother — he got frequently ribbed. No such thing as a secret in a small country town.

"There was funny lights all over the valley, out your way."

He shrugged, refusing to be drawn into any debate with

Spud. He'd seen a lot of strange stuff flying over the skies in the years he'd lived in the outback, but nothing had actually landed — as far as he knew.

"It's true," Will said, striding from the kitchen. "Gidday, Alex. How's things?"

"Good. You and Sev?"

"Okay." He smiled.

Alex studied him. Will's golden hair was now past his shoulders and he had a diamond stud in each ear. Since Will had fallen in love with Severin, he'd changed. He was more muscular, more beautiful. More centred. Though since Sev had arrived, Will had become aloof, a sadness beneath the playful façade. No matter how many times he'd asked what was wrong, Will never replied.

Will glanced at Spud. "I saw those lights, too. Like the aurora borealis, only green and purple. Quite a show."

"I went to bed early."

Spud snorted. "Yeah, who with?"

"Buzz."

"That mangy dingo? Lexie boy, you're slipping."

Alex snorted. Buzz was the only creature he shared his life with, apart from the kangaroos, emus, wombats, and echidnas on his property.

"The Bureau of Meteorology said the lights were just an atmospheric anomaly," Will said.

"That's a fucking lie," Spud replied. "Conspiracy to keep us from the truth that's out there." He whistled the theme tune from the X-Files.

Will grimaced. "You can't handle the truth." His gaze was troubled as he studied Spud. What'n'the hell did that look mean? Alex wondered.

"You want the usual, Alex?"

"Yeah, thanks."

Will strode to the servery and pulled out a cake from the fridge. Trudi worked on the espresso.

"So, Rasta, if you see any green men running around your

property . . ." Alex knew what was coming—Spud was predictable. "Green'd be okay, but maybe not so little, huh?"

"There's much to be said of quality over quantity, though you wouldn't know about either, Spud Murphy," Will said.

The café patrons roared with laughter, except the out-of-towners who glowered from their corner.

Will set down the coffee and cake on Alex's table.

"Where's Sev?" Alex asked.

"In Adelaide delivering another order."

"He drove? On his own?"

"Scary, ain't it?"

"Too right," he replied. Sev might be a fantastic baker, and a gorgeous guy, but he couldn't drive a damn. "Your sister and Tarix?"

"Fine. They're up the Top End on holiday. Suse is expecting twins, did I tell you?" William rolled his eyes. "I told Tarix I was gonna nobble him."

Alex smiled. "You and Tax! Always scuffling. The guy never leaves home, so it just goes to show how besotted he is, to go north with Susan."

"Yeah, I know. He's just a bloody shift . . . shit."

Alex noted the flush on his friend's cheeks, his look of horror. Whatever Will was going to say had suddenly changed to 'shit'. "Seen Mags?"

"Last week." Will nodded to the full length dresser on the far wall, laden with jars of Mags' kangaroo apple chutney and sticks of native sandalwood incense. "She left you a box of chutney and incense."

"The woman thinks I need mothering."

"Maybe you do, babe," Will said, smiling. "You know how Mags is."

Magdalen was another newcomer who had bought acreage across the valley, five years ago. She and Alex were neighbours, living twenty kilometres apart, separated by the gorge.

"I've brought the drawings," Alex said, reaching for his cotton rucksack.

"Finish your coffee. No rush. See me out back when you're ready." Will frowned at the chewed bottom of the bag. "Rat do that?"

Alex grinned. "Just Buzz. He got my rug, too."

"That's a dingo for ya!" Angrily, Spud pushed up from the chair and returned to his table.

Alex was one of the rare few in the town who was ever invited out the back into the private rooms and home of Severin and Will, a fact that miffed Spud big time. That he was third generation local gave him the right of entrance into any home, or so he thought. Will, fourth generation Christmas Creek resident, denied him access. Stalemate.

Laughing to himself, Alex skewered a piece of cake with his fork and lifted it to his mouth. The chocolate and toffee melted on his tongue. The cake was called Lover's Kiss. And it was the closest thing to a kiss he was likely to get anytime soon, he thought, sipping his coffee. Café Decadence served the best damn espresso. Even though Alex had his own machine and bought organic Arabica beans and ground them himself, the coffee just didn't have the extra oomph of the Decadence brew.

Finishing his coffee, he picked up his rucksack and pushed through the beaded archway leading into the private sitting room. Will was reclining in his comfy old chair, bare feet on a fat ottoman.

Alex spread the papers on the cedar table. "This is it."

Will stood up, his gaze flitting over the furniture designs. "Yes. I love it. And this one . . ." He pulled out another paper.

"Sorry, that's just a work in progress."

"I'll take it," Will said, gazing at the sketch of a baroque chaise longue.

"What . . ."

"Yeah. I'll give this to Sev for our anniversary. It'll be a year in October."

"I'm pleased for you, Will."

"And what about you, Alex, no sexy babe to hold you at

night?"

"Nope," he said flushing. He had arrived in the town three years ago, and Will had been the lawyer who had arranged the sale of his rural retreat. They'd been friends ever since. Even though Will was gorgeous, he didn't feel anything for the man, beyond the platonic.

"He'll come one day, lover boy." Will winked and walked away from the table to the safe hidden behind the ornate mirror hanging on the far wall. "Deposit. How much?"

"Nothing. It's okay."

"C'mon. You have to buy the wood and stuff, so you need a deposit."

Alex often sailed close to the wind when it came to finances. Will knew it, so did everyone in the town. Why sometimes accounts never reached him for goods and services he accessed in Christmas Creek. Why he, in return, anonymously left pieces of his woodwork, on doorsteps.

Will handed over a roll of hundreds. "Is a thousand enough?"

Alex knew from past experience that he couldn't win an argument against Will, or Sev, especially when they thought they had his welfare at heart.

"Come on out and have more coffee and something to eat before you go back to your lonesome hobbit hole."

Alex laughed. He'd built his eco house in the side of a hill, like the dug-outs in Coober Pedy. Living two hours out of town, behind the hills on twenty acres that overlooked the gorge, he rarely saw people. The road was terrible at best, a track that only a resolute friend like Will, or Mags, traversed.

He stuffed the money into his jeans pocket and returned to his table in the café. Will served him more coffee and a thick bagel overflowing with cheese and salad.

"I'll have the cupboard finished in maybe six weeks. The chaise . . . a lot longer. I'll have it done by your anniversary, though."

Spud chortled.

"See to that habit, Murphy," Alex said. "Snorting all over the place. You ought to be in quarantine. Maybe some more sheep dip for you, huh?"

Spud glared. There was no love lost between them.

"You sure you've had enough?" Will asked as Alex came to pay his account.

"I look like I'm starving?"

"Yeah, for lots of things." Will grinned at him. "I've got your order ready."

After paying the bill, Alex collected his akubra, rucksack and boots, while Will carried the assortment of Decadence Delights and Mags' box of preserves to the car outside.

"You still riding this heap?" Will demanded, eyeing the red Ford flat top. "There's so much rust on her, I can't tell what's paint and what's corrosion."

Laughing, Alex packed an esky with the chocolates and cake and climbed into his car.

Will shut the door, his hands resting on the half open window. "Come in for dinner next Wednesday, Sev'll be home. We want to talk to you."

"About what?"

"Stuff," Will said. "Private. Confidential."

"Lawyer stuff?"

"Kinda. And, if you do see any little Martians, be sure to let me know first, huh?"

"Yeah, sure." He grinned and reversed the vehicle out through the wrought iron gates.

Leaving town, he hit the dirt road and floored the accelerator, sending plumes of dust spiralling in his wake. He glanced at the blinding, azure sky. When would the rains come? Three months and not a drop.

One click from home and with the iPod blasting out a heavy beat, Alex saw the thing streak across the track in front of him. Just in time, he slammed on the skids, the truck slewing sideways.

What the hell . . . He got out and walked to the other side

of the track, standing on the rocky verge. In the distance he saw the skinny, golden slinking shape. His gaze narrowed. It looked like a goddam cat, but huge. A feral could grow big, but not that big. The cat stood under the shade of the mulga, eyes glowing with a strange mauve light.

Alex retreated to the truck and rummaged through his boxes of shopping. The cat looked starved. He dug up a can of salmon and pulled the ring, edging closer to the cat. It was fifty metres away, sides panting. It didn't run, but its every muscle tensed as he walked closer.

Alex put the tin down. "You want more, follow me." He retreated and watched as the cat picked itself delicately across the ground. It bent to the tin and ate ravenously. He opened more tins, leaving them under the saltbush beside the road.

"C'mon home," he said to the cat and drove off slowly, hoping the animal would follow. He watched in the rear mirror, but the cat wasn't there. Damn. He'd have to bring more food out to the cat, entice it closer. Maybe he'd get Mags to help — she was good at cornering strays.

Reaching home, and after putting away his groceries, Alex showered and donned a fresh pair of silk boxers. Listening to opera from his iPod, he ate his dinner under the pergola. The night was warm, the scent of sage, basil, and rosemary drifting over him from the herb garden.

Going to bed, he lay tossing and turning, his mind awhirl, re-drawing his furniture designs. He started as he heard a god-awful crying. Something was in trouble? He hoisted off the bed, padded to the French doors and walked out onto the verandah. In the distance he saw the cat, its head turned to the moon, wailing. He didn't know a cat howled like a wolf.

He put out a bowl of milk and went to bed, listening to the sudden silence. The silence that hurt the ears, the silence he loved.

ABOUT THE AUTHOR

Elizabeth Black writes erotica, erotic romance, speculative fiction, fantasy, dark fiction, and horror. Her erotic fiction has been published by several publishers. She also enjoys writing retellings of classic fairy tales. An accomplished essayist, she was the sex columnist for the pop culture e-zine *nuts4chic* (U. K.). Her articles about sex, erotica, and relationships have appeared in *Good Vibrations Magazine, Alternet, CarnalNation,* the *Ms. Magazine Blog, Sexis Magazine, On The Issues, Sexy Mama Magazine,* and *Circlet blog.*

Look for her on Facebook at https://www.facebook.com/elizabethablack.

Join her newsletter at http://eepurl.com/b76GWD.

Read her web site at http://elizabethablack.blogspot.com.